FALLOUT
BOOK TWO OF THE SEVEN KEYS SAGA

M.A. Brotherton

FALLOUT
BOOK TWO OF THE SEVEN KEYS SAGA
M.A. Brotherton

MABrotherton.com

For a Group of Friends that Let
Me Geek Out on Them

CHAPTER 1

"Alright, I'm here," Terry said as he ducked beneath the yellow-striped police tape. He balanced a cardboard tray that held two steaming hot paper cups of coffee in one hand while trying to keep the knots of his backpack's strap from cutting too deep into his shoulder with the other.

Once free of the obstacle, he was able to stand and shift his full focus to the old abandoned farmhouse. The stone foundation had collapsed years ago. The spray painted graffiti on the side of the building stood out in sharp contrast to the serene overgrowth of plants that had reclaimed the abandoned land.

Terry looked around and saw a tall, stone tower off to one side of the property. There was a large hole where some rocks had been removed with the words "Evil Awaits" spray painted beneath the opening. Below those words, Leigh was kneeling. Her face was a tight slate of concentration and her basket-ball orange hair, she kept pulled back in a pair of pom-poms, bounced as she dug in the dirt.

He waved to her, but she never looked up. She seemed completely oblivious to the activity going on around her. He knew it would be pointless to try to talk to her right now. So instead of going over to her, he turned his attention back to the man standing on the porch just outside an opening that, Terry guessed, had once served as a doorway.

Jared Slate was an older man, in his late thirties now, and Terry had gotten to know him pretty well in the last two years. Slate was leaning against one of the stone columns, his arms folded across his chest in a gesture that belied his ability to move. He wore a simple blue suit, dark enough to be mistaken for black in anything but direct sunlight. His black tie had spots of mud on it, and his eyes were like daggers as he watched Leigh work. Terry climbed the handful of stone steps and offered Slate one of the cups.

"You sure you can afford to call me out to look at every petty act of vandalism in the Midwest?" Terry asked, gesturing at the spray paint and litter. "Or did some Goth kid finally get eaten by the abominable snow man?"

"She called me," Slate said, motioning with the coffee cup toward Leigh. He pulled the lid off and swirled it around. "I called you after I got here and saw her going, well, Leigh on us. You want to get paid... you'll have to take it up with your other boss." He sniffed at the coffee then took a long, satisfying slurp. "God damn, you're my hero."

"So, what's going on? Found anything so far?"

Terry sat the second cup of coffee on the stone railing that circled the porch. It looked like it might be the only part of the structure that could hold the weight without collapsing.

He let the backpack slide down his arm, and sat it down on the floor by his feet. A muffled sound came from the bag and it began to unzip itself from the inside. A set of small, pointed fingers jutted out through the opening. The hands pulled on both sides of the zipper, giving just enough room for a knobby, bulbous head to pop up out.

Munindwade took a deep breath. "It smells like feet in there," the homunculus complained.

He started to climb out again, but only managed to flip the backpack over and get tangled in the rubber cords that hung down from the sides. He made a pitiful sound and looked up at Terry with big, sad eyes. "Little help?"

Terry leaned back against the railing and took a sip of his coffee. "Hey, you're the one that said you could do it yourself."

The homunculus turned his puppy-dog eyes to Slate and the hard veteran knelt down with a chuckle and pulled him free from the bags bindings. He sat Munindwade down on the stones beside the coffee.

"Hi, Muni. You keeping our boy out of trouble?"

Munindwade shrugged and brushed crumbs from the front of his hoodie. "He's gotten boring, Slate. He just sits around playing that video game with dragons in the title. But there aren't any dragon, Jared! There aren't any dragons!"

"It comes later in the game," Terry assured him.

Terry turned his attention back to Slate. "So, I know you didn't call me out here because Leigh wanted me to watch her dig in the dirt. So what's so great that she thought Meta-Crimes would be interested in the first place?"

"We got a call from some locals yesterday evening. At first, we just ignored it because, well, it's the Albino Farm, right? Kids come out here to smoke pot and play with Ouija boards. Really, not our territory."

Terry followed as Slate clambered down the stairs and started walking along the path that led deeper into the lot. "But, when neighbors reported that a lot of noise and some kind of light show was coming from out past the house; late last night SPD finally sent a patrol out here."

Slate led the way down the dirt drive and pointed with his coffee cup as they walked, "It's out there by the barn." he said.

Terry remembered the barn from a few years back when he used to hang out there himself. It was far enough back from the house that it had survived the fire. The stone walls and foundation were still in fairly good shape, considering they'd been neglected for almost thirty years. It still even had the wooden slat roof. Or at least it did the last time he was here.

But as he stepped into the clearing, Terry found himself staring at a scene of total destruction. The barn looked as if it had been smashed out by a wrecking ball from the inside. The roof was scattered across the field in several broken pieces and the smell of smoke wafted up from the rubble.

"What the hell happened... did somebody's meth lab explode or something?"

"That's what you're here for," Slate took another sip of his coffee, "You tell me."

Terry opened his mind and moved cautiously toward the rubble. "Do you feel that?" Terry asked, looking down at the homunculus.

Munindwade nodded. "Yeah," he said with a hint of awe in his voice, "Wait, I mean no."

"What is it?" Slate asked. He'd caught the glances being exchanged between the mage and his familiar, and didn't like the look of it at all. "Clue me in, Terry. I've seen that look on Stanley's face too often to be comfortable with it."

"Hang on," Terry said and took a step backward. He stepped forward again and repeated the motion a handful of times before kneeling down and pulling the knife from the pocket of his jeans. Scratching a line in the ground with one hand, he waved Munindwade over a few yards with the other. "You got it?"

Munindwade jerked his head up and down several times. He then scratched his own mark into the ground with his clawed hand. "Got it."

"So," Munindwade said, after doing some quick calculations in his head. "It's centered about 15 feet beyond the barn."

"What is it?" Slate repeated. He'd slid his hand into his jacket to rest on the gun in his shoulder holster under his left arm. "Are we being watched?"

Terry shook his head. "No, I don't think so. But staring here," He pointed at the mark he'd cut into the ground. "There's a null zone."

"What do you mean 'null zone'?"

"There's no magic here," Munindwade supplied. "In about a sixty foot radius, starting fifteen feet behind the barn."

"That's interesting," Slate said, heading toward the barn again. "Makes what I'm about to show you a hell of a lot harder to understand." He stopped just outside the barn and pointed at a hole about three feet wide burrowing down into dirt and rock. "It's down there."

Terry turned to Munindwade and grinned. "Guess who's going spelunking."

Munindwade dived behind Slate's legs and peered around his ankles. "Can I at least have a gun or something? I don't want to get carried off by a coyote again."

Slate looked at Terry with harsh, accusing eyes. Terry shrugged. "It was a golden retriever and she was extremely sweet. I actually think she thought he was a puppy."

"I got covered in slobber!"

"Okay, here." Terry gave him the pocket knife he'd used to mark the ground. "Now you have a sword. Go forth and be brave."

"Okay,"

Munindwade walked to the edge of the hole, with his pocket knife held to one side in an identical posture to Terry's own lazy stance. He peered down, then turned back around and held out his other hand. "I need a light."

Terry sighed and pulled out his car keys. He worked the small flashlight off the key-chain, clicked it on, and handed it to the homunculus.

"Just tell me what you find down there. Scream if it turns out to have teeth. I want enough time to get away." Munindwade gave him a dirty look that Terry returned with a toothy smile.

"Shoo." Terry said.

Munindwade turned and took a tentative step into the hole. He brandished the pocket knife before him and carried the flashlight on his shoulder like a bazooka. After a moment's hesitation he scurried down the hole, he and his light, disappeared from view.

Terry squatted down beside the hole to wait and Slate leaned against a tree a little ways away. They sat in silence for a while before Slate finally said, "You mind if I ask you something personal?"

"Sure, why not?" Terry said over his shoulders without pulling his eyes away from the hole.

"Munindwade, he's a piece of your soul, right?" Slate made it sound only vaguely like a question.

Terry hesitated for a moment before he answered. "Yeah, that's pretty accurate, I guess."

"So why isn't he a tiny asshole?"

That pulled Terry's attention away from the hole. He tilted his head back to glare at Slate. He curled his nose and blurted, "Fuck that's mean?"

Slate held his hands out in a placating gesture. "No offense Terry, but you're usually a dick to most people. Muni's, well, nice, courteous and sweet."

Terry rolled his eyes and shook his head slightly, "After I brought you coffee, too."

"I'm just asking the questions everyone else is thinking," Slate said. "No need to wad your panties."

"Honest answer," Terry said a moment later.

"Yeah."

"I have no idea." He turned back to the hole and leaned down, sticking his head inside. "Hey, assface, you found anything down there yet?"

There was a shuffling noise and Munindwade popped up out of the hole. "Terry, you should come down here and look at this."

"What is it?"

"A containment circle," Munindwade said. There was a hint of fear in his voice. "A scary one... and it's broken."

CHAPTER 2

Terry squeezed his way down the tunnel. It widened slightly at the far end, giving him enough room to pull himself out into the open, spherical cavern. He slid down the side and his light caught something glinting on the walls. Coming to rest, in the center of the bottom curve, Terry pushed himself up and held his light steady to examine the silver sigils that had been embedded into the limestone.

The hooked glyphs ringed the chamber in a spiral that began at the very center of the ceiling and looped down to end just below his feet. The only place the pattern was broken was where the tunnel, that he had just come through, was cut into the stone wall.

"This is... complex," he said, looking up at Munindwade standing in the tunnel at the edge of the hole. "Have we seen anything like this before?"

The symbols and patterns seemed familiar to Terry, but he wasn't able to recall having ever seen a chamber like this. Summoners in the Order had used smaller, simpler, versions of the same pattern while making deals with spirits. That was something he was extremely familiar with. He'd even used a couple of these symbols in his own contracts.

9

"We've never seen it," Munindwade said. He hopped down from the ledge and slid along the wall in the same way Terry had. "But, we know what it is."

Terry looked down at the homunculus and was surprised to see genuine fear in the creature's face. Munindwade often complained and whined, but he didn't generally feel actual fear. He was more or less indestructible. As long as Terry was alive, or he was able to find another person to bond with, Munindwade would continue to exist. Sure, the gangly body and over-sized head were flesh and bone, but the actual essence of the homunculus was pure spirit.

Terry flashed the lights across the sigils again, trying to read them this time. The embedded incantation didn't make that much sense to him. It wasn't a rote he was familiar with, and he was sure that it wasn't one he'd just forgotten. He shook his head. "So, what exactly are we looking at here?"

"A prison," Munindwade said. He had his knife out again and his eyes darted back and forth nervously, "A bad prison and we don't want to be here if the prisoner comes back."

Terry opened his mind fully to the emotions in the chamber, trying to get a read on exactly what had been kept here. He could feel his own curiosity reverberating off the chambers wards, and the small, nearly panicked ball of emotions at his feet, but there was nothing else.

"If something had been trapped down here for over a hundred years, Muni, we'd be able to sense it. If it was strong enough to make you that jittery, we'd be able to sense it coming from a mile away."

10

"Terry," Munindwade reached up and pulled on his pant leg.

Terry rolled his eyes and knelt down. He held out his hand and Munindwade placed his palm down against it. A small jolt, like a mild static shock, ran up Terry's arm and stung the back of his brain. A memory rolled forward. It wasn't his memory. It wasn't even a memory in the way most people would think of memories. But, it was vivid and powerful.

"Oh," he said. He looked around at the symbols on the walls, recognizing them with the perfect clarity of someone else's mind. "Son of a bitch."

"Yeah," Munindwade said. "Can we go now? I need help getting up the wall."

"It doesn't make sense." Terry mused to himself. "There's no way it would have fit through that hole."

"Well it did. Now let's go."

"How did it break the binding?" Terry reached down and picked up Munindwade by the back of his hoodie. "Memorize these patterns, Muni. We might need them."

"Terry, I already have. They're order sigils. A Binding Arcanum, for an elemental lord. He probably wasn't very nice, either, because Order mages don't just go burying nice guys in a rock tomb for years with no good reason!"

Munindwade fidgeted in his grasp, and kept repeating "let's go," over and over again until Terry finally tossed him back up to the opening.

"Go on ahead and tell Slate what we found. I need to figure out how it broke the ring before I can come back up. It's gone now. I doubt it'll be coming back here to its prison cell."

He watched Munindwade scurry up the little hole and turned back to the sigils on the wall. Terry pulled his phone from his pocket and turned on the camera. Slowly and methodically, he followed the pattern down around the room until he had made sure he'd gotten all of it. Then, just to be sure, he did it again.

Something wasn't adding up the way it should. There shouldn't have been a way for the elemental to break free. An air spirit bound inside a stone prison would have a hard time gathering any power. Even if it had, the sigils would have absorbed it almost immediately.

A rustling noise and a few low curses came from the tunnel. Terry spun and pointed the flashlight at the opening, causing another low curse to come from the orange-haired head poking out through the opening.

"Christ, Terry, get that out of my eyes," Leigh protested.

She blinked several times after he'd moved the light, and then slowly lowered herself down from the opening. She blinked a few more times when she'd reached the bottom, trying to force her vision to adjust to the darkness of the hole.

He watched her as her vision slowly returned and saw the moment when curiosity and surprise cracked into the expression on her face. She pulled a small notebook from the back pocket of her jeans and started to scribble notes furiously. She would pause, now and then, to point with the pencil's eraser in small sweeping motions to identify each different section of the ward.

"What do you think?" Terry asked after a few minutes. "How did it break the spell and get free?"

She made a harsh shushing noise and continued her notes. After filling three or four more pages, she closed the spiral bound tablet and stuck it back into her pocket. She tucked the pencil behind one ear and crossed her arms over her chest. She examined him slowly and then made a gesture with her hands and shrugged her shoulders. "Okay, Go."

"How do you think it broke the spell?" Terry asked, gesturing at the tunnel opening. "Did it fail? Was it time released? What?"

Leigh's eyes glazed over slightly as she took in the room again. She squeezed her eyes shut and rubbed at her temples. "I don't think it did break out." She pointed around the room, gesturing at the empty space. "If something in here dug its way out there, where's the extra dirt?"

"So, if it didn't break out, then something had to break in." Terry said.

Leigh shrugged. "That's what I've got. Come on, I've got something you need to see outside." She hopped up to the hole and snagged the edge, pulling herself back up into it.

Terry took one last round of pictures and stuck the phone back into his pocket. He looked up at the hole. A sylph could probably squeeze through any size of opening, but how did the opening even get there.

13

Terry crawled back out of the hole in the barn a few minutes later. His face and hair were now covered in mud, and all he really wanted to do at the moment was get home and take a shower. Slate was waiting for him on the other side and he grabbed Terry by the hand to pull him up out of the hole.

"So, little man says we've got a jail break." Slate said. He offered Terry a box of baby-wipes, and Terry happily accepted them. "Some kind of giant moth?"

Terry wiped his face and hands, then pulled out a few more wipes and did it again. "Something like that. A Sylph. An air elemental, but this wasn't a normal one. It was corrupted."

"So, someone locked it in a hole under a barn in the middle of town?"

Terry shrugged. "Wasn't a barn here when they did it, or even a town for that matter. The land probably came fairly cheap once it was here though. But, it still doesn't explain the null zone. When the big bad wolf huffs and puffs and blows your barn down, it uses a lot of magic to do it. This entire area should be lighting up the mystic Geiger counter like Chernobyl right about now."

"I told you," Leigh said defensively. "It didn't break out. Someone or something broke in."

She pulled a small red stone from her satchel and held it out to Terry. It was covered with black flex and there were fractured lines running

14

along the surface. It leaked small amounts of raw magical power. Something about it made his stomach twist. "What is it?"

"I think," She hesitated as a pained expression crossed her face. She shook her head in a familiar, practiced gesture before continuing. "I think it's a battery."

"Yeah? Like a magic battery? I've never heard of anything like it." He examined it a little closer. "Have you ever seen anything like this before?"

"Not that I remember," she said quietly. Her eyes were glistening with early tears, and Terry could sense the pounding migraine crashing into her. She paled a little and caught his look. "I'm gonna head home and see if I can find out anything about it on the net."

"Okay," Terry said. He stuck the stone in his jeans pocket. "No offense, Leigh, but you look like you might be coming down with something. Don't overdo it, okay. I'll check with the magi-tech guys at Meta-crimes and see if one of them can do the research part. That's what they are there for anyway, right Slate?"

Slate nodded. "Those guys get nerd boners every time Terry lets them look at anything. They'll fight each other over the chance."

"Okay," Leigh said, starting back down the path towards the road. "Just give me a call if you find anything."

"I will," Terry said. "Promise."

He watched Leigh walk away for a moment to make sure she was going to be alright and then turned to Slate, "I'll meet you at the office in about an hour. I want to get a shower and some breakfast before I come in."

Slate gave him a salute in response. He was already on the phone with the techs. Terry took the opportunity to slip back down to the burned ruins of the house. He put the stone in one pocket of his backpack and helped Munindwade climb into the main compartment.

"You didn't say anything," Munindwade said as Terry slid the pack back over his shoulder.

"I don't have anything to say yet. We don't know for sure." Terry said quietly. He gathered up the cardboard tray and coffee cups and started back toward his car. "I'll have to check the registry to make sure."

"We don't need to check anything," Munindwade blurted. "Leigh made that stone, Terry."

"We know that, Muni," Terry told him. "But she doesn't."

CHAPTER 3

Terry stopped outside the door to his office and fished his keys from his pocket. He fumbled with them for a few seconds before managing to get the right one. He slid it into the brass deadbolt, gave it a quick twist, and dropped it back into his pocket. He took a deep breath and pushed open the heavy wooden door, stopping only briefly to pull the paper messages taped to the frosted glass just below where his name and the word "SPECIALIST" were painted in blocky, black letters.

He flicked the lights on with his free hand and tossed his backpack into the chair, eliciting an angry squeak from the homunculus riding inside it. Munindwade pulled the bag open and managed to climb out of it onto the back of the chair without dumping himself out, a feat that made him pump one fist in triumph.

Terry snagged him from the back of the chair by his hoodie and sat him down on the desk, pushed the backpack to the floor under it, and flopped down. He grunted as something hard pressed against his leg, and he fished the broken stone from his pants pocket and tossed it casually to the desk beside the homunculus.

"I don't get it," Munindwade said. He poked at the stone with one sharp finger. "How can someone just forget that they made something?"

Terry shrugged. He leaned back and put his feet up on the desk and folded his hands behind his head. A quick glance at the clock told him he probably wouldn't have any interruptions for another hour while the rest of the meta-crimes guys were out to lunch. "Everyone forgets some things. Leigh just forgot more than most."

"So, why don't you tell her? I tell you when you forget to turn off the stove." Munindwade stopped poking at the rock and walked across Terry's desk to the old wooden lock-box on the corner. He hopped up onto it and leaned forward to rest his elbows on his knees and his chin on his fists. He looked at Terry through the tops of his eyes in a twisted semblance of a pout and waited for an answer.

"We don't know exactly what happened to Leigh, but we know it was bad. Real bad." He dropped his feet to the floor and leaned forward to match Munindwade's eye level. "All people have things they have to block out. There isn't enough room inside our heads for everything our brains could remember. We have to let some things go." His voice took on a sad tone. "And sometimes, there are things that happen to us that we don't want to remember. There are things that happen that hurt to remember. We're just going to have to trust David when he says that we shouldn't pry into her past. We'll figure this thing out without her."

Munindwade nodded solemnly and hopped back up from the lock-box. He walked over to the edge of the desk and looked back at Terry. "I don't forget anything. There's lots of room in here." He tapped the side of his head. "And I'm a lot smaller than you." He dropped down off the desk to the rough carpet and scurried over to the dorm fridge stuffed between a three drawer file cabinet and a folding metal chair. Grabbing a piece of rope tied to the handle, he slung it over his shoulder for leverage, and pulled the door open about half way. He climbed inside and came back a moment later with a can of store-brand soda. "You want one?" He asked.

Terry shook his head. He ignored the homunculus and instead pulled open the box on his desk. He began to pull out the small collection of tools he kept in the office for the rare occasion when his skills were actually needed. The kit was sparse, hardly anything compared to the stockpile of magical tools he'd inherited from his former mentor and the last specialist the Secret Service had employed, Stanley White. These were his secondary tools, the ones he'd crafted himself back when he was still training with the Order, back when there was an Order to train with.

He looked up when he heard the click of the soda can followed by the hiss of carbonation. "Humans are weird," Munindwade declared, then, using both hands to lift the can, chugged the soda in one long pull. He sat the empty can down and let out a belch that sounded a little like the cross between a mouse-squeak and a fog-horn.

"You're weird," Terry said. He picked up the smooth piece of black chalk from his tools and cleared a section from the center of his desk. "You don't need to eat or drink, but you do, constantly."

"I like soda," Munindwade retorted. "And cupcakes. Soda and cupcakes."

"And hot dogs," Terry muttered. He carefully drew a circle on the surface of his desk with the chalk and sat the stone in its center. "Basically anything made of nitrates and sugar," he paused, "or covered in yogurt. Freak."

"Things need to remember what they are, Terry." Munindwade lifted the empty can up over his head and pushed it into the recycle bin beside the door. "Everything has a memory that defines what it is, except humans. Look at you! You can barely remember anything before me. That's a quarter of your life just gone."

Terry picked up the six inch metal office ruler from his tools and painstakingly balanced it on one end in the circle of chalk. "Why would I want to remember all that time I spent screaming in starvation and shitting myself?"

"That's not everything babies, do." Munindwade replied. He walked to the corner of Terry's desk and climbed up the leg to bring himself back to the surface. "Don't forget the feathers," he said, emphasizing the word "forget."

"I'm gonna use the sand," Terry said dismissively. He picked up the six vials of colored sand from the kit and sat them out beside the ruler. "Don't shake the desk, it's a bitch getting that thing to stand up like that."

"Just because babies don't know language yet doesn't mean they don't have deep thoughts." Munindwade walked over to the collection of tools and picked up the spool of waxed dental floss. "You're looking for this."

"You're a deep thought," Terry said with a grunt and took the floss. He wrapped a long strand around his finger and broke it off with his teeth.

"You don't get it," Munindwade whined. "I am my memories. I am what I know. If I forgot any of it, I wouldn't be anymore. There is more to life than just being a body."

Terry looked at him with flat eyes. "Muni, you're being serious. It doesn't fit you well. Do the sand, I've almost got the knot ready to go."

Munindwade took a handful of sand from each of the jars and poured it inside the circle, careful not to break the surface. Terry finished tying the last of seven loops in the floss and then carefully laid it so that each loop touched one of the piles of sand. The last loop was stuck down inside the crack in the stone.

"Okay, that should do it, back up."

Munindwade backed away from the contraption and Terry touched the circle lightly with the tip of his right hand. He closed his eyes and focused his mind on balancing the various energies. A tiny, imperceptible spark slid from his finger tip into the circle.

Slowly, the sand started to shift inside the circle, each colored pile rising slightly in response to the small bit of magic he had pushed into them. The circle flared for a second as the ambient energy inside was burned off. Terry spoke a few rhythmic words under his breath and the floss tightened around the stone. The sand began to rise as the energy

21

draining from the stone separated along the floss and flowed into each grain.

"Okay," Terry said as he watched the sand rise. "Take the measurements."

At that moment, the door to his office banged open and Chad backed in carrying a bag from Baker's Dozen Donuts in one hand and a massive energy drink in the other. The ruler fell over without any hesitation, breaking the circle and sending sand flying into the air in all directions.

"Son of a bitch," Terry moaned. He looked up at the clock again and rounded on the teenager with a scowl. "Shouldn't you be in class?"

Chad shrugged. "Yeah, I'm done with that." He kicked the door to Terry's office closed and held up the bag. "Hey Muni, want a cruller?"

Munindwade hopped excitedly down from the desk and ran over to sit at Chad's feet. "Yes, please!"

"What do you mean you're done with class? It isn't a half day, is it Muni?" Terry stepped around the desk. "Was there a gas leak or something?"

"No," Chad said. "I just dropped out."

CHAPTER 4

"I don't understand," Terry said as he sat back down in his chair. He eyed the chubby teenager wearily. "You can't just drop out of school. You go to school, Chad. That's what sixteen-year-olds do."

Chad pulled a donut from the bag and handed it to the homunculus. Munindwade snatched it with both hands and scurried under Terry's desk, chirping excitedly. "Not anymore I don't. I decided to drop out. It doesn't make any sense for me to keep going, Terry. I've learned more from you than any of my teachers and I already have a job, right?"

"Not if you drop out of school," Terry said through clenched teeth. He closed his eyes and took a few deep breaths. It wasn't so long ago that he'd been in Chad's shoes. It had been hard to see the value of a high school diploma in a world that was literally tearing itself apart around him. He rubbed at his temples, pushing the headache away by sheer force of will. "I'm not going to pay you to fuck up your life, Chad. I gave you a job so you could help Lydia out with gas and errands. You go to school. You can decide to not go to school once you've graduated... from college."

"It sucks, Terry!" Chad sat the bag down on the desk and pulled a large, jelly filled from it. "You know how much it sucks. You dropped out!"

"I dropped out of college, after fighting a war, Chad. And it was a mistake for me, too." He grabbed the bag from his desk and looked inside. There were a few cream-filled long johns resting in the bottom. "You're trying to bribe me into agreeing with you?"

Chad shrugged again and sat down in the metal folding chair. "No," he moaned. "I thought you'd understand. I'm your apprentice. I'll do what you've taught me to do. Do I need a GED to fight monsters?"

Terry pulled one of the long johns from the bag and eyed it. "No," he admitted. "You need a High School Diploma."

"You're not my dad, Terry." Chad said. Terry glared at him, but didn't say anything. Chad had known exactly what string he was pulling.

"No," Terry finally said after a few heartbeats. "I'm not." He sat the long john back in the bag, no longer interested in it. "How's he doing, anyway? You haven't said anything in a while."

"He's doing better," Chad said between mouthfuls of donut. "They put him on some kind of new medicine. I mean, he's never gonna get out of there, but sometimes he's almost like himself again."

A strong pang of guilt closed the conversation. Terry turned away from the teenager and began putting his tools back in the lock-box in silence. Chad watched him work for a bit, finishing his pastry. After the silence had hung in the air long enough to drive him insane, he finally spluttered, "It's not your fault!"

"It is, but thanks for thinking that," Terry said. He closed the box and locked it. He stood up and went to the file cabinet. "I mean, yeah, he was already pretty gone, but I pushed the buttons that threw him over the edge."

"The bastard almost killed my mom," Chad said. He stood up and Terry realized how close to his own height the kid had gotten in the last couple of years. "You might have put the bomb in his head, but he's the one that pushed the button. All he had to do was not be an asshole, Terry. He couldn't do that for even a week. He's getting help now. He needed it."

Terry pulled open the file cabinet and fetched the carbon fiber training swords from the top drawer. "I know. But, I should have done something different. Remember that lesson, Chad. The human brain is a delicate piece of crap. It is not rigid enough to mess around in there without knowing what you're doing. We'll both leave it to the experts, right?" He offered one of the swords to his apprentice.

Chad took it and nodded. "Alright, I don't have an interest in going spelunking in anyone's psyche anytime soon, that's for sure. Heck, I can barely get my own head clear."

"Good. Then today we're going to practice combat rotes. I hope you're ready to concentrate and not all hopped up on sugar and niacin." He grinned as he headed out the door. "Come on Muni, you can keep score."

"Do you need me?" Munindwade said from under the desk. "I think I can rebuild the meter while you're gone and get a good reading."

Terry gestured out the door. "You just want to eat all the donuts. Let's go."

He stepped into the hall and right in front of a short, thin man in a lab coat. Maxwell Roderick jerked his head up in surprise just before slamming into Terry. He reached up with one hand and pushed back the greasy black hair from his face and adjusted his glasses.

"Oh, hey hotshot," he said, "I was just coming to see you."

"You sure you want me to keep humiliating you in public, Roddy? I mean, if I keep breaking all your toys, how will you get any of the other kids to come play in your yard?"

"I don't know, Terry. I guess I could try being a giant douche-nozzle. It seems to work for you." Roderick replied. He stepped back to let Terry come out of the office and pointed at Chad behind him. "Shouldn't he be in school?"

"Yes, he should," Terry said. He looked over at Chad with a level gaze. "And we'll talk more about it later, and with his mother. If he can convince her that he doesn't need a diploma, I guess I can show him exactly how much excruciating work goes into being a spook hunter."

Chad's jaw dropped and he started to say something, but Roderick held up his hands. "Don't look at me, Chadwell. I have two, count them, two PhD's. You're definitely looking at a pro-school kind of guy."

"Okay," Terry said. "I think the kid gets it. You're just stalling now anyway. Let's see what your hunk of crap can do."

CHAPTER 5

"Looks like you got it off its tether; you find batteries big enough to power this thing?" Terry said. He paced in a circle around the massive construct. Roderick's special project, Tiny, stood just shy of eight feet tall. The body was proportioned more or less like that of a professional body builder with massive hulking shoulders. The skin was made of thick polymer clay that gave it the appearance of being cut from solid stone. Terry stopped his pacing in front of it and placed one palm on the chest plate. He reached out with his mind but couldn't feel any currents running through it. "How'd you do it?"

"Trade secrets," Roderick said. He sat a black impact resistant case on the folding table to the side of the sparring ring. "I came across some research that sent me in a whole new direction. It's pretty advanced." He popped open the case and pulled out a thin, ceramic board covered in a series of small tiles. "But, he's definitely up to the challenge this time."

Terry nodded. "So you fixed the thing with the arm?"

"I think so." He slid several of the small tiles around the board and the eyes of the construct flared to a dull green glow. "I re-enforced the structure with poly-carbonate plating. Like on the space shuttle."

"Didn't they retire the space shuttle because it was going to explode?" Chad asked. He stood a way off to the side, eyeing the construct.

"No," Terry said, failing to mask the annoyance in his voice. "You'd know that if you went back to class."

"Probably not," Roderick added. "I don't think they teach about the space shuttle anymore. Public school isn't what it used to be."

"Not everyone can be a trust fund baby." Terry walked away from the construct to the far edge of the sparring ring. He took some time to stretch and warm up his body, watching Roderick running the construct through a series of diagnostic checks out of the corner of his eye. "It's moving a lot better today."

"That thing is enormous, Terry." Munindwade said. He was sitting just outside the ring, taking everything in with his over-sized eyes. "Don't let it hit you. I bet it'll hurt if it hits you."

"Thanks, Coach. I'll keep that in mind." Terry turned back to the ring and pointed toward the construct. "Any weaknesses?"

Munindwade shrugged. "The armor is going to be hard to break with a fake sword." He tapped at his face. "Eyes? Maybe blind it?"

"I'm not sure how well that will work with the remote standing over there." Terry gestured with his chin to where Roderick was explaining the tile board to Chad. "We need to study more mechanical engineering, Muni. Things like this didn't happen when the Orders kept a strangle-hold on magic. Now, every geek with internet access is going to be building magi-tech. We're living in the dawn of a new age, Muni, and we're dinosaurs now."

"You should get an iPhone. Or better, you should get me an iPhone."

"I have data limits, you know." Terry picked up the training sword and rested it on his shoulder. "Alright, Roddy, time's wasting. Let's get this done so I can show the kid some tricks."

"Yeah, yeah, all talk." Roderick pushed a tile forward on the board.

The construct lumbered forward, its eyes changing from green to red as it charged. The floor rumbled with each hulking step as it began to pick up speed. Terry didn't hesitate. He dove forward, planting one palm against the floor and letting out a slow breath. He spun on his hand and pushed off against the floor with a gust of wind that drove him feet first into the oncoming brute. Pain shot up his legs as he hammered both heels into the thick chest plate and bounced off, crashing onto his back with a thump.

"I fixed the stabilizers in the legs," Roderick shouted. "It won't just fall over again."

One huge fist rose up and came crushing down at Terry's face. He managed to push himself to one side and roll away from an impact that splintered the wood of the floor.

"Christ, Roderick! You trying to kill him?" Chad screamed. "I thought this was a sparring match!"

Terry pushed himself to his feet and hopped back a few yards from the construct. "It's fine, Chad. There are a lot bigger things out there." He leaped to one side again as the construct came streaking toward him for another blow. He spun, dragging one foot along the ground beside him and holding out his left hand. "Ascunde Vederii," he hissed, pushing a bit of will out through his extended palm. The surrounding temperature dropped significantly as the humidity in the air began to thicken into fog. "Okay, Muni, I'll try it your way."

"Not so fast," Roderick chimed from the sideline. Before the fog was able to form more than a thin haze, he flipped one of the tiles on the control board. The construct stopped moving, folding forward into a crouch. Heat wafted off of it in sharp waves, burning the fog off in a thick steam.

Terry put one hand over his face and stumbled back, trying to blink the tears from his eyes. He felt the pressure around his chest as the construct grabbed him. It lifted him into the air and swung him toward the ground. Terry's mind reacted on instinct, warping the air beneath him to soften the impact against the ground, but the rock hard palm pushing against his chest drove the air out of him. It leaned its weight forward, pinning him in place.

Terry reached out and slapped his palm against the floor twice.

"Woo," Roderick cheered as he slid the tiles back down on the board. The construct let go of Terry's chest and stood back up, its eyes going dark. "Victory for Science!"

Terry slowly pushed himself to his feet, taking in long deep breaths. "So you're what, One and Five?" He walked over to the edge of the ring and handed the training sword to Chad. He picked up a bottle of water and chocked it down. "I want a rematch."

He sat the bottle of water on the ground and turned to face the construct. Reaching up to undo the chain from around his neck, he pulled the old black iron key from under his shirt. He gripped it in his right fist and held it out to the side. A sharp bite of power ran through his arm as it extended out into the form of a broadsword with sharp, pointed tines in the shape of a crescent. "I want to see how it stands up to field conditions."

Roderick shrugged. "I've been studying your fancy stick, Terry. I think Tiny can handle it." He moved the tiles again and the construct flared back to life. Its eyes immediately transitioned from green to red, then flared into a burning crimson. It lurched forward, swinging its fist in a wild haymaker.

Terry stepped to the side and brought the blade up in an arch that smashed into the polymer clay flesh and sent a shower of spark cascading across the sparring circle. The massive fist forced its way through his guard and clipped him across the shoulder, sending him sliding back across the waxed floor. Terry bounced himself back to his feet and surveyed the damage.

A few chunks of the false flesh had been ripped free,

exposing the smooth black surface of the inner armor. He'd managed to cut a scratch into the poly-carbonate plate and a weak white glow leaked out. Terry let himself grin.

"You've re-enforced the armor with a composite order weave," he said over his shoulder. "Good move."

"Thanks," Roderick said. He slid another tile forward. "But get your head in the game. I've got it on full offense."

"Good, burn some power." Terry waited as it charged at him again. The construct barreled forward, arms spread to grab him in a bear hug. He stepped back, bent his knees, and leaped into the air, focusing on the air beneath him to push him up and over the construct. He flipped in the air, grabbing the construct by the head with his left hand and forcing the blade down between the clay flesh and poly-carbonate armor beneath. He jerked hard against the blade, cutting a large hunk of clay from the back.

The construct jerked, trying to shake him, but Terry clung to its back, striking the plate repeatedly in the same place, drawing a deep, glowing line in the armor. "Time to go to sleep," he said through clenched teeth as he put one palm against the line of leaking energy. He took in a deep, sharp breath and the power in the construct began to fade. Terry pushed himself off its back and walked slowly away, pulling a line of power out and away as he did. The white energy slowly wrapped its way around his left arm. He jerked his hand one last time, and the construct stopped and collapsed to the ground.

Terry held his hand up and let the energy dissipate into the room. "Start the count," he said to Munindwade.

"How did you do that?" Roderick was already standing over the construct, scanning it with what looked like a Geiger counter. "You completely locked up the armor. It can't move? That's...," He looked up at Terry, "Impossible."

CHAPTER 6

"That's what I do," Terry said with a sigh. He leaned back in his chair to put his feet up on his desk. "It's years of training and intense mental discipline." He grabbed the can from the desk and took a swig. "Seriously, Roddy, I thought you studied this stuff."

"Okay, I get that. I do, but that was, something else entirely." Roderick had a notepad out and was jotting down ideas as they came to him. "I re-enforced the armor with white crystal energy-"

"Law," Terry corrected.

"It's energy that came from white crystals. Anyway, you shouldn't have been able to disrupt it just by, what, touching it?"

Terry took a deep breath and blew it out. "No, not by just touching it. Look, Evocation is a discipline, one of many. It's kind of the Order of Midnight's specialty. There's a lot of history here and I don't know that I can just explain it all in fifteen minutes."

"So how many people can do that? Is it common knowledge, or is it something only you guys can do?" Roderick's voice had taken on a distant, mechanical tone.

"There are one-hundred-thirty-six Midnight Order mages left in the world," Terry recited. "All of them are trained in Evocation. It's a skill though, so some are better than others. I don't really know what other orders learn, or how many of them are left, but Slate's tracker shows less than a thousand of us in the United States."

"Interesting," Roderick looked up from his notebook. "I've never thought of it in that context. I've always assumed you were more or less one culture."

"Well, we were." Terry stood up and tossed the empty can into the recycle bin. He walked over to the fridge and pulled out another one. "Want one?" When Roderick nodded at him, he tossed the can to him and grabbed a second.

"Think of it like this," Terry said. He clicked the tab on the can and let it hiss. "You were in a fraternity, right?"

"Sigma-Chi," Roderick affirmed.

"So, you know how different Fraternities are all basically the same."

"That's not true."

"Okay, that, right there. That's the difference between the Orders. To outsiders, it might look like they're all the same, but they're actually completely different. And, like the Greek System, we were all pieces of a bigger, stronger community... until we started killing one another."

"I have to warn you," Chad said from the door. "If you get him started like this, you'll be going all night. He likes to make sure everyone around him knows that he's smarter than they are."

35

"Well, I've got quite a bit of data to process anyway. I want to get at the readings from the gym. Besides, I'm supposed to be supervising the techs. They're overhauling some of the old equipment that got pulled out of storage."

Terry grinned and looked at his apprentice. "Chad can help you with that. Can't you, Chad?"

Chad shrugged. "I guess," he moaned. "I was hoping to get to go out in the field with you and Slate."

Terry waved a hand. "No, that isn't going to happen. The way I see it, if you're going to drop out of school so you can work for me, you've got a couple of options. You can stay here, and do Roddy's bitch work, or you can go and spend time gaining first-hand experience with a legendary magus. Sure, the farm might be full of back-breaking labor, but think about it. First hand training from Harley McFinn himself. I'm sure Grandpa has all kinds of things he could use you for."

"I can help you! I can handle myself in the field. Come on, Terry." Chad pleaded, but Terry just shook his head.

"One little apocalypse and you think you're ready to play with the adults? Please." Terry glared at Munindwade sitting on his desk before the homunculus could point out his own hypocrisy. He wasn't doing this by his own choice; he'd been strong-armed into it. "The other option is to go back to school and get your diploma. Maybe even go to college and be something that doesn't involve knowing the best way to get blood out of your clothes."

"Pro-tip," Roderick added, "club soda is not nearly as effective as everyone claims." When everyone turned to look at him he held out his hands in surrender. "I do research for the Secret Service. You think it hasn't come up?"

Terry gestured at him. "Get a job like Max's. Have you seen the car he drives? You aren't going to ever afford that on any job you can get without a GED. That's the kind of thing a college degree gives you."

"Well, to be fair, the trust fund helps." Roderick grinned. "But I do make a comfortable living without having to worry about getting eaten by dragons or shot by crack-heads. It's not about the money, though. I do it for the science."

"Is what you do considered science? I thought you made magic gizmos?" Chad's voice carried a tone of skepticism that caused Roderick to put a hand to his chest in mock indignity.

"Magic gizmos? Magic Gizmos!" He stood up, throwing his hands in the air. "Just because you Order stooges believe in some sort of random esoterica doesn't mean that the rest of the world can't categorize it away. The magic you use is simply a manipulation of the fundamental laws of the universe. Gravity, Strong and Weak magnetic fields. You know, physics."

"I don't know that's true," Chad protested. "I mean, it doesn't feel like I'm altering magnetic fields."

"What have you been teaching this kid?"

"The truth. Magic can do anything if you know how to make it work." Terry sat back, watching the explosion of consternation rolling off

Roderick in huge waves. He smiled at the thought that Chad might be back in school by the end of the day.

"Just like physics," Roderick almost shouted. His face had turned red and a little of foam was forming at his mouth, but he was already running out of steam. He stopped, took a deep breath, and said, "At least theoretically."

"From the Earth to the Moon!" Munindwade shouted. He pumped one fist into the air, caught up in the rant. "Large Hadron Collider! IPhones!"

"Damn straight," Roderick shouted, raising his own fist in solidarity. "How many mages have gone to the moon?"

"Six," Munindwade said excitedly.

Roderick turned to him with a pointed glare. "Thanks, Muni. I was making a point, though."

"Science is cool and so is magic," Munindwade supplied.

"Yes, thank you. Thousands of years of human history have been split by this rivalry between 'wizards' and 'scientists.' If we'd all been working together this entire time, imagine what we could have accomplished."

Terry just nodded. He could think of a couple of examples of what happened when magic and science played together in the same sandbox. Atlantis was a pretty good example, and there was a reason that it didn't exist anymore. As it was, though, he agreed with Roderick's point.

"So that's what you do," Chad said. "You make magic robots and stuff like that?"

Terry could see Roderick start to protest, but he twitched and stopped himself. "In layman's terms, yes. I make magic-technology. Magi-tech, for lack of a more appropriate word, but really, it's all the same."

"So, you can teach me how to make magic robots, too?" Chad's eyes lit up with the idea.

"No," Roderick said, crushing the kid's dreams with one syllable. "But, I can show you some cool stuff and teach you a couple of neat tricks. I went to school for twenty-two years, kid. You don't just learn to build constructs in an afternoon."

Chad shrugged. "Good enough."

Roderick wrapped one arm around the teenager's shoulder and said, "I'll show you a new ballistic vest that makes wonder boy's super-man jacket look like skate pads." He led the kid out of Terry's office and off down the hall.

Terry sat back down in his chair and put his feet back up. He looked over at Munindwade, sitting on the wooden lock-box, staring longingly at the open office door. "You want to go, too, don't you?"

"He's going to the research lab, Terry! The research lab!"

"Fine, go." Terry waved a hand dismissively. "Keep an eye on Chad, and don't eat any books!"

Munindwade bounced up from the wooden box and scurried down off the desk and out the door much more quickly than his size should allow. He spun around Slate's foot as he stepped into the frame, made an excited squeak and rushed off down the hallway.

Terry pointed at the manila folder tucked under one of the agent's arms. "Hey, Slate. That the report from this morning?" he asked.

Slate pulled his eyes off the homunculus's mad dash down the hall and held up the folder. "No," he said with a solemn shake of his head. He handed Terry the report and sat down in the folding chair. "We've got another crime scene."

CHAPTER 7

The downtown restoration project had brought a lot of the old, abandoned warehouses and factories to new life as expensive, upscale lofts. They all followed the same neo-industrial design standards, filled wall to wall with exposed brick, air ducts, and shiny appliances.

"Now this is the kind of place I could get into," Terry thought, although he would never admit it to anyone. "That is, if I had piles of money I could burn just for the fun of it."

Slate pushed open the single metal door at the top of the outside stairs and the two of them stepped into the apartment. The interior was immaculate. The apartment was unoccupied. The model home furniture, in reclaimed wood and brushed steel, shone like it had been freshly polished. The apartment itself already took up the entire top two floors of the building. But the open, flowing design made it seem even larger.

The lower level was more or less one long room, running the width of the building. There was a small, but efficient, kitchen tucked against the back wall. The rest of the space was divided into zones by the type of furniture grouped there.

The area just inside the door contained two small, brightly upholstered chairs and a wooden couch all aimed at the huge fifty-inch television on the wall. It all flowed nicely into the large wooden table, that looked like it had once been a barn door, and its four wooden chairs in the center of the room. A set of narrow stairs, just off the back of the kitchen, led to the upper level and presumably to a bedroom and bathroom of some kind.

"Are you sure this is the right place?" Terry asked. He looked around the loft and soaked in the view. Yes, this is exactly the kind of place he could find himself living in, given enough money. "This is definitely lacking the creep factor usually associated with haunted buildings."

Slate thumbed through the folder and handed him a stack of black and white photos. "These are from a few months ago, before the renovation. Definitely a little more your style... all cobwebs and broken glass."

Terry looked through the pictures, checking all the surfaces for any signs of graffiti that might suggest someone other than hobos or bored teenagers had been using the building. Nothing in particular caught his eye, but the images had been printed off an historic district renovation's website, and were designed to sell the city on the project. They'd been taken to highlight how much of a hazard the old building had been, and why it needed to be restored. They were not high quality images.

"It's the life of a professional, Slate. So, what exactly happened?" As far as Terry could tell, the place was spotless. It was the perfect model

42

apartment. He opened himself to the room and sensed nothing but the ambient energy of the surrounding city. It was a blank canvas waiting for a new owner to come in and make it a home.

Slate lifted his chin toward the stairs at the back of the apartment. "Up on the roof," he said, and led the way up. He opened the folder as he walked, double checking the facts of the report. "Uniformed officers were called by the downstairs neighbors this morning. There was no sign of forced entry and as far as the Realtor can tell, nothing is missing. The neighbors reported, and this is a quote, 'Loud banging noises, like the dude was practicing to be in Stomp, you know, man.' Responding officers did a quick glance around and pushed the case up to us when they found the scene on the balcony. Report says they didn't touch anything. The officer looked out through the door, saw the scene, and left without disturbing it."

Slate stopped outside the roof access door and tucked the folder back under his arm. Terry waited for him to continue but, after a few moments, impatience got the better of him. "What's on the roof, Jared?"

"You tell me." Slate pushed the door open and waved for Terry to go through. "After you."

Terry rolled his eyes and stepped up onto the rooftop balcony. He took a deep breath and drew in as many of the details as he could with a quick glance. The patio was a wooden deck about twelve feet wide and fifteen feet long. A banister made of flat wooden slats ran the outside perimeter, just tall enough to lean against comfortably. Plants and flowers sat in pots every so often along the banister, the kind you would see in a magazine photo shoot for better homes and gardens.

The patio furniture was mostly untouched, except for the shiny new gas grill lying on its side next to a broken planter. Both were only a few feet from a broken section of the balcony that had been smashed inward by some great force. Splintered wood chips were strewn across the patio. Terry's gaze followed the pattern of wood chips across the deck until his attention fell on a mangled body sprawled beneath the white patio table.

He let out his breath slowly and moved out onto the porch, side-stepping the little pool of blue-green blood staining into the wood. He walked around the edge of the porch, taking his time in examining a series of round holes that appeared to be burned into the wood.

"It wasn't human," Slate said from the door. "So, what was it?"

Terry pulled his phone from his pocket and took pictures of the holes, then pulled up an app to measure the angle of the burn. He measured several of the holes. Each of them was a perfect two inch circles. He chewed at his lip, then tapped out a quick message and sent the pictures off.

"He was a kobold," Terry finally answered with resolve. "A house spirit or live in family."

Terry steadied himself and went over to the corpse. He knelt down and raised the face to examine it more closely. The smooth gray skin was unbroken by any hair or blemishes. Terry closed his eyes and choked back the rage boiling up inside of him. "That's what I thought."

"What is it?" Slate had pulled out his notepad and was making notes. "Kobolds are like, what; little dragon guys that make traps and things, right?"

Terry shook his head. "That's in D&D. No, kobolds are house spirits. Like, uh, you've heard about the cobbler that had the elves that made shoes at night?"

"Yeah, they'd come out when he was sleeping and finish his work for him so he wouldn't die of starvation."

"Yeah, so that's what kobolds are. We might be in a different part of the world, but the old folk lore holds. I wouldn't be surprised to find out that they are more yippy and aggressive here in the USA, though. You know how The Folk are. But there's the million dollar question. Where are the other two?"

"What do you mean? Why would there be two others?"

"At least two more. This one wouldn't be living alone, even in a brand new home like this." Terry forced himself to look away from the face.

He began rifling through the kobold's clothes, checking pockets and folds. Tucked inside the loose wrapped shirt, he found what he was dreading. A brown stone, flecked with black, cracked along one side.

"Terry, I know you enjoy playing Mr. Knows-it-all, but come on, man. I'm the only one here, and we both already understand that you know this stuff better than I do."

Terry stood up and met Slate's eyes with a grimaced expression. "Because it's a fucking child, Slate. You got it now? He was a fucking toddler and someone broke him in half." He tossed the stone to the agent. "Two. That's two."

Terry started toward the door, a nauseous pain growing inside him. "We're looking for a magus from Unbroken Light, just like Carter fucking Neil."

He moved quickly toward the apartment door, his eyes flaring with the anger boiling up inside him. Just before he reached the door though, Slate slid in front of Terry and the agent's steady, cool eyes locked into his. The unpolluted calmness on Slate's face forced Terry's anger to subside enough for him to regain his composure.

"How do you know?" Slate asked. His voice was calm, placid, and almost hypnotic.

"The two inch burns," Terry pointed over at the holes in the railing. "During the war the Galahads started carrying these little poles about yeah long," he held up his hands about a foot apart in demonstration. "They don't use a lot of offensive magic, but those things, they just burned everything they touched. No matter how hard we tried to come up with a counter, nothing could stop the blast."

"Couldn't someone else have gotten their hands on them? They can't be that hard to find. You're accusing a couple hundred survivors of murder just because they happen to have been part of a group that owned a weapon five years ago. That's like accusing every cop of being a murderer because someone got killed with a 9-millimeter."

Terry shrugged and Slate grabbed him by the shoulder and turned him around. "Look at the kobold, Terry. Did you find a hole in him?"

Terry shook his head. "No," he said solemnly. "He looks like someone crushed his spine. It wouldn't have been easy. But, someone trained in using magic to make themselves incredibly strong wouldn't have a problem doing it."

He turned back to Slate. "It fits," he insisted. "White Knight mother-fuckers killing monsters because they don't understand." Slate didn't stop him this time as he left.

Terry's phone vibrated in his pocket about halfway down the stairs, and he read the message. There was another possibility, one he wasn't ready to consider yet. The death sticks were a tool. They'd be hard to use, but Slate was right. Someone with the right set of skills would be able to get their hands on one. Or build one from scratch.

Outside, he stopped at the top of the metal stairs leading back to the parking lot. He took a cigarette from his pack and lit it. The burning smoke roiled through him, helping him push down the anger and fear that had been building inside him. He flipped the cigarette into the air and watched the sparks splatter as it hit the pavement below.

Terry headed down to his car. He'd made his decision and now it was time for action.

CHAPTER 8

Terry put the car in park and lit one last cigarette. He'd parked a few houses down from the classic single-story ranch home with brown shudders clashing against yellow siding, smiling at the thought of how much it must be driving Gabriel insane they hadn't been painted yet.

Terry had been avoiding Suez and Gabriel since they'd gotten their own place. He hadn't wanted to add to their burdens. They had enough on their plate with the problems inside the Community, and that had nothing to do with planning a wedding.

He leaned back in the car seat and waited for the activity to die down. The house was never fully quiet, Sue had people coming and going pretty much from sunrise to sunset. That was the cost of being the head of a small nation. Terry was reminded again how thankful he was for not having managed to stumble into that particular role.

As the last group left the house, Terry pulled himself out of the car and tossed the long black coat over one arm. He would need to put it on if he had to deal with any of Sue's assistants, but he was really hoping to avoid that. The coat was nice to have, a symbol to remind him what his actual job is. But, it was a coat and Southern Missouri in early summer was not known for being cool and comfortable. He walked along the driveway and then followed the stepping stones that were set into the grass up to the front door. An envelope was taped to the door, Terry's name, written in Sue's flowing handwriting, on the outside.

He pulled out the note that was folded neatly inside. It read, "About Time, Bitch. Come on in." He rolled his eyed and opened the door.

"Hey, Sue? Gabe? Anyone home?" He called, closing the door behind him. When he didn't hear a response, he stepped into the living room. Suez had done pretty well for himself the last couple of years. There were quite a few members of the sovereignty that had more than their fair share of money. Although the salary that he'd managed to draw wouldn't be considered huge, it was definitely not-too-shabby by Springfield's standards. Terry sat down in the fluffy white chair and started to thumb through the piles of wedding magazines stacked on the coffee table.

"I'm thinking you and David will be in mermaid cut dresses and matching sequins pinned in your hair," Gabriel said as he flopped down on the couch. "Something strapless, of course, but not too much cleavage, just enough shoulder to attract interest."

Terry shrugged and tossed the magazine back onto the table. "I've always thought I'd look good in a bustle."

"So, what's up? Haven't seen you in weeks, then about an hour ago, Sue told me to tape that letter to the door and went out back to light up the grill. What brings you all the way down here to Chez Moi?"

"I need help," Terry admitted. He held up the coat in explanation. "I don't know what to do."

"Come on," Gabriel said, pushing himself to his feet. "We're out back, but officially off duty." He pulled Terry to his feet and headed toward the kitchen. "Leave the coat, you don't need it." Gabriel pulled open the sliding glass door and the smell of charcoal wafted in from the patio. Terry followed him onto the covered concrete slab. Suez was standing beside the grill, scrubbing at the metal with a wire brush. Gabriel walked over and gave him a hug from behind, whispering in his ear. He nodded, and turned to smile at Terry.

"Hi, Terry," he said with an unexpected tone of sheer excitement. "We have steaks and cold beverages. As soon as David and Trish get here, it'll be a real party."

Terry stood in the door, eyeing the array of camp chairs, coolers, and folding tables covered in picnic foods. "I can't stay that long, Sue. I just came-" Terry started to say, but Suez cut him off.

"You are going to eat my meat, Howard, and you're going to like it. Then, you're going to spend at least three hours with your friends, relaxing and enjoying nice weather. You will have a good time. You will not complain." He hung the wire brush from the side of the grill and turned, hands on hips, to stare at Terry with sharp eyes. "Do I make myself clear?"

"Yes, Your majesty," Terry answered. He stepped out onto the patio and lowered himself into one of the collapsible camp chairs. "I do still need to talk to you, though."

"It can wait." Gabriel pulled a bottle from the cooler and handed it to him. "Sue knows why you're here. He's just being a bitch." He pulled his own bottle from the cooler, popped the cap and sat down next to Terry. "Cheers, and happy birthday."

Terry opened the bottle and clinked it against Gabriel's. "My birthday was in April," he said with a smile and took a drink. He sat the bottle down on the concrete at the foot of his chair. "But, I guess this is the first time I've seen you guys since then. Sorry."

Suez shrugged and laid steaks on the grill. "We get it. You're deep in the brooding Terry hermit mode. It happens." He sat the empty plate on the table, and bent down to kiss Gabriel on the forehead. Terry dropped his eyes to the side, and Suez made a chuckling noise. "Besides, if you spent too much time with us, you'd die from blushing."

Terry shrugged. "It's not you guys. I'm not good with anyone showing affection. Trust me."

Suez went back to the steaks. "You're coming to Iowa, right?"

Terry shook his head. "I don't know if I can. I don't know how you're getting away for two weeks. I've only been out of the office a few hours, and I'm sitting at about fifteen messages. If I was gone for that long, I'd come home to a pile of paperwork deep enough to bury a village."

"You indulge them too much. Why are they even coming to you? Tell them all to piss off and eat your ass with a spoon." Suez flipped the steaks. "You got to have boundaries, and you're too busy keeping them safe to deal with their petty bullshit."

51

"Well," Terry said, "I could say, 'You know there's this guy you can call. He actually gets paid, by you, to deal with your problems'"

"You could, but it wouldn't do you much good," Gabriel said. "Our public number gets forwarded to an assistant with instructions to tell them to piss off and call you. Just turn your phone off."

"I can't tonight. Munindwade is babysitting Chad while he's with Roderick. I need to stay available in case of an emergency."

"You worry too much." Gabriel stood up and put his empty bottle in the trashcan beside the door. He started to sit back down, but Suez grabbed him by the hand and kissed him, causing Terry to look away again. In the year since they'd moved out of his apartment, he had gotten used to seeing stoic, distant Gabriel again. The private moments of intimacy had been common once, but now, he just felt like an intruder. He knew it was a stupid feeling. This was family, but it was still there.

"They're here," Suez said in a falsetto, and pushed Gabriel toward the sliding glass door.

CHAPTER 9

"You didn't tell me he would be here," Carrie said as she stepped through the sliding glass door. She glared at Terry, lip twisted in an angry grimace that oozed a slime of hatred and pain. David stepped through the sliding glass door behind her and put an arm around her shoulders.

"Of course he'd be here, why wouldn't he? We don't pick sides between friends," he said. He slowly guided her away from the open door, leaving room for his new girlfriend, Trish, to come out onto the porch.

Inside, Terry groaned. It was bad enough to be holed up with his ex, but there was something about David's pregnant girlfriend that set the hairs on the back of his neck to rising. It wasn't that she was a bad person, or that they even clashed on beliefs. There was just something that he couldn't quite explain that made him irritable in her presence.

"I should go," Terry said to Suez. "I don't want to be the drama." He started toward the gate in the fence to the side of the house, but Gabriel caught up to him, and dragged him away from the others.

"It's time to grow up, Terry. You have to accept that you are both going to be in our lives. I admit, once upon a time, I was on your side. What happened between the two of you was, well, horrible. But, you've got to let the past go. You have to step up and be the bigger person. If you don't want drama, don't make drama."

Terry glanced back at Carrie. She was standing just outside the door, arms folded over her chest, a look in her eyes that could melt iron. He huffed out a sigh and let his shoulders slump in defeat. "Okay, I'll try."

"Good." Gabriel turned back to the group, with a wave of his hand. "You guys hungry?"

Carrie slid her stare from Terry to Gabriel and pointedly said, a little sullen, "not anymore."

"Carrie," Suez warned. "Play nice."

A commotion at the gate drew Terry's attention away from the quiet, heated discussion that he was sure was almost identical to the one he'd just had. He walked around the corner of the house to find Chad carrying a small stack of pink and white boxes, Munindwade riding on top. He quickly flipped the latch on the gate and held it open for the kid and caught Munindwade as he leaped from the boxes to Terry's shoulder.

"Why are you so mopey?" The homunculus asked as soon as he'd arranged himself to keep from falling. "What happened?"

"Nothing," he grabbed one of the boxes from Chad. "Let me help you with that." He looked down at the white silhouetted outline of a short, plump woman wearing a chef's hat on the cover and smiled. "Okay, you can take the rest of these over there, and I'll just hold on to this one."

"Mom said not to let you walk off with a whole dozen again." Chad walked around the house and Terry followed behind, sharing a grin with

Munindwade. "She said she hid one coconut cupcake in every box, and there's no way for you to know which one it is."

Munindwade made a gagging noise. "Might as well make them toenail flavored."

"Amen."

They sat the boxes on the table with the rest of the food, and followed in line as everyone filled their plates. The meal was awkward at first, but it didn't take long for the mood to shift as good food hit everyone's stomach.

The evening faded into nostalgic conversation and Terry found himself sitting against the fence at the far side of the yard, smoking a cigarette as far away from the pregnant woman as possible. Munindwade sat beside him, idly pulling up grass and weaving it together.

"You're mopey," Munindwade announced after a few minutes. "It's boring."

"Sorry."

"I exist to point out things you already know," Munindwade croaked. He looked over at the group sitting on the patio, talking and joking. "Remember when you weren't the outsider?"

"I've always been the outsider," Terry moaned. The self-pity annoyed even him. "I can handle it. It's what I'm here for."

"Maybe," Munindwade said. "Maybe not. Maybe you're just being a big baby."

"Why are we still her, Muni? Something is going on out there, and we should be stopping it. Instead, we're having a barbecue? It's not right."

"All work and no play makes Terry a giant ass-face. What else would you be doing? Waiting for something to happen? Beating up informants? A stakeout? What's the key telling you to do?"

"Soulbinder hasn't said anything to me in weeks. He gets like that." Terry adjusted the chain under his shirt, a reflexive gesture whenever he thought about it. "And the other one has never said anything to me. Ever."

"But Scary-head always says something when big things are happening, right?"

"I suppose," Terry admitted.

"So, obviously, nothing big is happening."

"That's very logical."

"Live long and prosper." Munindwade held his hand up in the Vulcan salute.

Terry's phone buzzed in his pocket. The text message from Slate just read "Three" and had an address attached.

"Shit." Terry pushed himself to his feet, picked up the homunculus, and slung him over his shoulder. He stopped at the edge of the patio. "I've got to go," he said with a wave. "Duty calls."

"Already?" Suez whined.

Terry shrugged. "We don't have the manpower for me to take an entire night off. Half of the cops in this town got sent to prison, remember? Having a hard time recruiting new ones, which," Terry took a deep breath.

"Sue, do I have to do this formally? We need help. We need people that can just, you know, be cops."

"I'm sorry, Terry, but we don't have anyone," Suez looked over at Gabriel with a quiet plea in his eyes. "I don't have the authority to just strong-arm anyone into doing it. It's not like we have our own cops or army. That's what you're for."

"Alright, I get it." Terry pushed away the disappointment. "In that case, I really do have to go." He waved goodbye and headed inside to get the things he'd left in the living room. He was almost out the door when Gabriel came out of the kitchen, slipping on his jacket. Terry eyed him curiously, but Gabriel walked past him out the front door.

"What are you waiting for, Howard? We got work to do."

Terry grinned and followed him. A sense of rightness flowed up in his chest as he fell into step beside the taller man. "Could be dangerous, you know. Might be as big a deal as Neil."

Gabriel nodded. "Yeah? Sounds a lot better than planning a wedding."

CHAPTER 10

"Have I told you how much I hate being here?" Terry asked as he and Gabriel made their way down the sidewalk to the beach. "Especially at night?" The wind coming off the lake was unseasonably cold and bitter. A chill started to seep into him as he walked, adding to his dread.

"About three times in the last fifteen minutes," Gabriel assured him. "But, you keep coming back, so, I assume it's all bravado."

The tripod-mounted spotlights in the distance shone down like a beacon on something huge. Terry wasn't entirely sure what it was at this distance, but it was easily the size of a large van. He didn't think there was anything that large in Saddy's territory. If there was, it couldn't have been dangerous. Lake hags were about as territorial as it came in the spirit world, and this one wasn't a lightweight.

"One of these days, Gabriel, she's going to force me to hold my end of the deal. It'll be bad." Terry said as they got closer to the water. "You have no idea how bad."

"One day you're going to have to tell me exactly what deal you made with her," Gabriel said. "It sounds like a great story."

Terry shrugged. "Not much of a story. I was alone, cold, hungry. I couldn't even catch a fucking fish to save my life. She found me and made sure I had something to eat. In exchange, I give her things she can't get."

"Like candy?"

"And other things." Terry stopped as they reached the ring of lights pointing at the form covered in canvas. Several of Roderick's techs were running around the area, taking measurements and collecting samples. Slate stood off to one side, watching them work. He looked up when he saw them approach, and Terry could see the pain rolling off his face when he saw them.

Slate walked over slowly, barking a command for the techs to take a break. He and Gabriel exchanged a handshake, and he looked back over his shoulder nervously. "I'm glad you brought him with you," he said quietly.

"What is it?" Terry stepped up to the canvas and held out a hand to feel at the form without touching it. "Cold and wet."

"You should know that she was a fighter, and didn't go down easy. There's a lot of destruction up and down the beach." Slate rubbed his hands together uncomfortably. "Gabe, you should stick close. He's going to need to talk."

Terry rolled his eyes and pulled the canvas clear of the form lying on the beach. Pain rocketed through him, guilt and frustration creating a sharp cocktail in his chest. He forced himself to detach from the emotions and accept what he was seeing. Before him, a massive gray form lying broken on the beach. The burns and tears in its flesh leaking a steady fog of dissipating power into the air.

It was the body an old woman, her flesh torn away in places and her thick, brown sea weed hair lying in clumps beside her. Terry starred into the huge, ancient black eyes of the catfish face. He forced the regret down and fought to keep the fear from rising up in its place.

Aunt Saddy had been an elder spirit. She'd existed in the Ozarks for as long as there had been water here. She'd lived through wars, dams, highways and party boats. She'd fought beside guardians of the veil on a dozen occasions. There were legends about her.

But now, she was lying motionless on the beach of Lake Springfield, her power slowly fading away into nothing.

Terry reached out with one hand and rested it against a whisker the size of his wrist. It twitched violently at his touch and he jumped back. The black eyes focused on him. The thick dry lips began to move and her voice came out in low steady rasps. "What you on 'bout, boy?"

"Hello, Aunt Saddy," Terry said, relief washing away fear. "You're not going to die on me, are you?"

"Boy, I'm as old as the river." A soft choking noise came from her throat and she blinked in her unnatural way. "I ain't got time for no death tomfoolery."

Terry looked back at the wounds, watching the mist spilling from them thicken and burn away faster than they had before. "Don't use up your strength talking to me, Saddy. I'll get you back in the water with your daughters and you'll be fine in a few months."

Her eyes flickered back and forth. "No, boy," she smacked her lips. "I'm a dried out ol' lady. I shoulda done passed when the river became a lake. I stayed, and now I got a bargain to uphold."

"You've held up your end," Terry said. He reached out and touched the fish face again. "You can pass on. I'll be fine."

Saddy made another chocking noise and spit out a chunk of thick, black goo. "I ain't talkin' 'bout me, boy. You got to keep your word now."

"You get back in the water, and I will." Terry felt the heat at the back of his eyes and had to blink away tears. "I promise."

"You can't worm away from me." Her eyes hardened and narrowed on him. "You ain't got a hook that can snag ol' Saddy. You think I'm some nixie, running 'round in the water, not a thought in my head? I'm the river, boy. I'm ancient and eternal. So quit your jabberin' and pop them ears open."

Terry stood up straighter and nodded.

"Good. Now, you take that magic stick of yours and you claim me."

"Saddy, I can't-"

"You promised me, boy. You promised to bind with me when the time came. That was our deal. Now you claim me, and I'll help you find the sumbitch that did this and put 'em in a pine box."

"Who was it?" Terry felt himself ask. "Who did this?"

"The Artificer. Needed power." She sighed as the mist began to pour off of her skin. "I'm the biggest fish in the lake. Wanted to mount me on a wall." Her words became clipped and pained as she spoke, and she let out a little gasp after each word. "Now, do it boy. I ain't got the power to keep on jawin'."

Terry nodded. He pushed back the tears from his eyes and pulled the key from around his neck. He didn't summon the sword. He didn't need it. He just touched the key to her forehead. "Now maybe I'll finally catch a fish."

"Boy, you'll grow gills and swim with my great-granddaughters before your hooks start lookin' tasty."

She smiled and the light faded from her eyes. The mist leaking from her body began to glow with a faded silver light as it gathered into tendrils and pulled along the key and into his arm. A cold, shivering sensation tore its way through him and gathered at his chest. It hung there for a moment, like a heavy ball of ice, and then began to spread through his veins to the rest of his body. He turned back to face Slate and Gabriel standing a few yards away and brushed the tears from his eyes.

"Okay," he said quiet, his voice fierce. "I'm going to find this mother fucker and I'm going to bring him down." He walked past them, headed back up the paved path to his car. The rush of power in his body mixed with the anger and grief, and he felt himself shaking. He got to the top of the path and leaned against his car to light a cigarette. It took him several tries to get the lighter to ignite, but the smoke burned its way down his throat with a powerful, reassuring pain.

The lake stretched out below him, quiet and empty. It was a grave now; a tomb that will always be haunted by memories. The lake is a little bastion of nature's power surrounded by the advancement of humanity, and in its own time, will call a new guardian to serve it. It will only be a matter of time until a new spirit, a new hag, moves in to claim it. It might be one of Saddy's daughters or it might be something completely new.

Terry dropped the cigarette butt and ground it out with his heel. He'd deal with those problems when they came. For now, he had a killer to find, and time was running short. Three points made a pattern.

"Terry," Gabriel said as he came up the path. His voice was quiet and firm, his sermon voice. Terry lit another cigarette and grunted, looking away from his friend.

"Okay, you don't want to talk. That's fine. I'll be around when you're ready, but Slate told me to give you this." He handed Terry a clear plastic bag, inside was half of a blue stone, black flecks mottling the outer surface. The center was a burned out hole about the size of Terry's thumb.

He stared at the stone for a few minutes, letting the implications swirl around inside his head. Finally, he stuffed the baggie into his jacket pocket, looked up at the sky and let all of his frustration and anger out in one long, croaking scream.

"Fu-u-u-u-u-u-u-u-u-uck!"

CHAPTER 11

Terry bashed his fist against the door to Leigh's apartment. The frustration fueled adrenaline high had started to wear off, and now he only had a lingering sense of anxiety. He needed answers, and he was going to get them. He didn't care about playing nice anymore.

Gabriel stood behind him, a grim expression masking his face. Terry knew what the look meant. He didn't like what they were doing. He understood why they were doing it, but he didn't like it. It was the same expression he'd worn whenever Terry had broken one of his religions taboos on magic.

A shadow crept across the peep-hole, and the sound of locks being undone rattled from inside. A moment later, Leigh opened the door to let them in. A wave of incense flowed out through the door like a wall of patchouli and cinnamon. Terry forced himself to not check her eyes for lucidity and stepped inside without saying a word.

Leigh squinted at him as he passed. "Have you been crying?" she asked. There was a hint of surprise and worry in her voice, tinged with just a bit of fear.

He ignored her, instead he focused on the familiar apartment in a new way. The small collection of trinkets, tokens and charms that she'd kept in stock over the years was stacked neatly on the shelves or placed into every nook and cranny. They were all barely artifices, novelties mostly. They were the kinds of things tourists bought from the gift shops at haunted mansions or stoners bought from the head shops in town. He knew she had been capable of more once. She still had a small armory hidden somewhere. It had the kind of tools that people spent real money on, and yet, he'd never known her to sell any of them, and there had been opportunities. She'd provided him with access to some of them on occasion. He had no reason not to trust her.

"What's up?" She asked, a little sliver of panic rising off of her. "Is everyone okay? Did something happen to Sue?"

"Sue is fine," Gabriel told her calmly. "Everyone in the circle is fine, and still at the house last time we saw them."

"Have you been down by the dam lately," Terry suddenly asked. He turned back to face her. "Maybe done some fishing?"

The accusation was harder than he'd intended, but the anger was pushing at his temples and he couldn't seem to shake it back down. He pulled the stone from his pocket and held it up to her. "Recognize this?"

Leigh's eyes fell on the stone, and she shook her head. "It looks like the one I found out at the Springlawn farm, only blue. Why?" She balked when she saw his eyes narrow. He stuffed the stone back in his pocket and turned away from her again. "Terry, I haven't been to the lake in weeks, and the last time I went, I was with you and David."

She sat down on the futon without looking and began to rub at her temples. "What's going on? Tell me!"

Gabriel sat down beside her and put an arm around her shoulders. "It's okay. We're not accusing you." He looked up at Terry standing on the other side of the room. "I'm not accusing you. We just need to understand what the stones are for. We need to know why they keep turning up."

"I can't," she sobbed into Gabriel's armpit. "I can't."

Terry rounded on them. The anger had crept up and grabbed at the sides of his brain. He didn't want to play good-cop-bad-cop with his friend. He didn't want to have to do that. He just wanted the answers.

"Yes, you can, Leigh!" Terry's rage crashed in waves inside his mind and he felt himself lose control. A flicker of power lashed out of him with the words and Leigh began to convulse.

A sudden, powerful fear pushed its way through the anger and a different instinct took over. Terry found himself rushing to her side, pulling her away from Gabriel and laying her down across the futon. He grabbed the wooden incense burner from the little table and pulled the stick free. He cleared the soot as best he could with his palm and shoved it down between her teeth as she began to foam at the mouth.

"What did you do, Terry?" Gabriel shouted from beside him. There was panic there, and Terry didn't have time to calm him down.

He reached into his pocket and handed Gabriel his phone. "Call David, Now."

The instinct was still pulling at him, and he followed it. He didn't have much in the way of medical training but he knew there was more he could do. He laid one hand on her forehead and took one of hers in the other. If David could do this without any formal training, he could too.

He took a deep breath and closed his eyes. The barrier, that divided her aura from his, faded and the two melted together. It wasn't dissimilar to forming a gate in the veil. Her fear came rushing into him, not as a separate sensation, but as a part of him, his hands were afraid and in pain. He tried to follow the sensation back to its source, but his vision began to blur and a heavy pounding erupted inside his head. Everything went white, and he felt himself fall to the floor.

CHAPTER 12

The pain wracked him in torrents, and Terry had to force his mind to keep it separate from his own emotions. He felt the barrier slowly rise into place, and floated for a few moments in comfortable darkness. When he opened his eyes, he found himself standing in a dark room made from cut stone walls, lit only by the soft glow of a single large sigil on each wall. A figure moved in the shadows of one corner, polished black skin shining in places. Soulbinder stood quietly, his attention on the corner opposite himself.

Terry peered into the darkness there. A second figure sat in the corner, arms curled around her legs, head buried in her knees. Her orange hair hung down around her face in dirty, dingy strands. A low moan rose up from her, and Terry rushed to her side. Before he could reach out to her, Soulbinder's voice boomed through the room, sending every atom in Terry's body humming in response.

"Don't open Pandora's Box."

Terry spun on him, clenched fists hanging at his sides. "Why not? She's in pain. I can help her."

"You are causing the pain." The onyx guardian pushed itself away from the wall and stepped into the light coming off the walls. "Hubris," it said, gesturing to the walls. "Humanity's greatest weakness, in raw form."

"Bullshit. I can help and I should help."

"Does being able to do something mean you should do it?" It shrugged and nodded to Liegh's huddled form. "Do you think she wants you to see this?"

"I don't care."

"Because, you're too proud to admit when you're ignorant.' Soulbinder thundered.

Terry turned back to Leigh and knelt beside her. She was whispering something to herself, and he had to strain to hear it. "It's wrong. It's wrong." She just kept repeating it over and over.

He put his hand on hers and she flinched away, drawing herself tighter into the corner. "Leigh, it's me. I'm here to help."

"She doesn't want your help, bearer. Trust me on this."

"Leigh," he squeezed her hand tighter. "I didn't mean to do this. Please, let me help you."

Her eyes jolted up, burning in a pale blue as she stared into him. "You didn't. You shouldn't be here."

"Neither should you," Terry pleaded. "Stand up. Help me find an exit."

"I have to stay here, Terry." A spiderweb of energy began to spike out from her, spreading in a series of symbols and glyphs that arched across the room. He watched as they began to grow and split, burning formulas and equations into the stone. "I can't leave. I can't take it out."

Terry took a step back as the formulas spread farther and farther over the walls. Each line split into dozens of smaller, more intricate lines. He couldn't understand what any of it meant, but he recognized the simpler equations as basic physics and magical theory. As he watched, they continued to expand across the room, spreading to fill every inch of the stone in writing so small and complex that it became impossible to decipher.

"What are you showing me?" He asked in a tone of awe mixed with desperate pleading.

"This is good," Soulbinder said, examining a section of the wall. "This would work."

"Of course it works," Leigh snapped. "It always works. It always works."

"Oppenheimer would be impressed," Soulbinder mused. "You are become death, destroyer of worlds."

"You think I don't know that? You think I don't know what I've done?" She turned her cold stare on Terry and her face melted from the hard lines into a quiet pleading. "Please, you can't ask me to remember this. I locked it all up. I hid it away. This can't come out."

"What do you mean, become death?" Terry asked. "That's from Bhagavad Gita, right? Is this about the stones? What do they do, Leigh?"

"Power." She grabbed him by the shirt and forced him to look at her. "It was about power, always about power. I needed more. I needed to make a miracle happen."

"I don't understand. You have to explain it to me." Terry felt another presence in the room, something warm and friendly. It wrapped around him like a gentle hand and began to pull at him. He recognized it. David had arrived and was fixing his mistakes.

"Please, Leigh. It's important. Lives are on the line." He struggled as the energy soothed him back. The more he fought against it, the more subtly it managed to move him back.

Leigh stood up and turned to the guardian. "Is it true? Are there lives at stake?"

"There are always lives on the line, artificer. The question is which lives are more important than other lives." Soulbinder stepped back into the corner. It faded into a patch of blackness and disappeared completely.

The room began to grow fuzzy and Terry held out his hand. "Come on, we need you for this."

She looked down at his hand, nodded, and grabbed it with her own. The green energy spread out over both of them, and Terry felt everything fade. His eyes opened as the pain flooded back into his head. David knelt over him, one hand on his chest, the other pressed against Leigh's. He moved his hand away from Terry, recognizing without looking, that the danger there had passed. He concentrated on Leigh, the green light focused on her head.

Terry pushed himself to a sitting position and let out a low groan. "Is she okay?" He asked, looking over at the still unconscious woman lying on the couch.

'Yes," David said with a sharp voice. "You're going to have one hell of a headache though, but she's going to be okay."

CHAPTER 13

"What the fuck were you thinking?" David shouted. He paced back and forth across Terry's perch on the small balcony. His face was red, flushed with anger, and he occasionally smashed one fist against the palm of the other hand for emphasis. "You can't just go diving into someone's head. Anything you want to heal, you have to pull out first. If you don't know how to shield yourself, you're doing more harm than good."

Terry let him rant. It wasn't anything he hadn't heard before. He'd even given that speech to Chad more than once. Magic was dangerous. It could be unpredictable if you don't know exactly what you're doing. Doing something without being ready always has unforeseen consequences. He knew that, in theory. But it was hard to keep in practice, especially when you're watching your friend choke on her own tongue.

The door opened behind them and Gabriel stepped out onto the porch. He silently lit a cigarette and offered one to Terry. "I put her to bed. How long do you think she's going to be out?"

David's rant boiled out of steam with Gabriel's question, and he leaned back against the railing. "It's hard to say. She had some serious trauma in there. She could be down for a few hours or a few weeks. I've never seen anything like that before. It was like a piece of her psyche had just been cut out and walled off."

He turned to Terry. With his rage gone, his concern took over, and he started examining his friend for any signs of damage. "How do you feel?"

"You remember the night we drank the pineapple bombers until we couldn't stand up?" Terry asked. He pressed the heels of his hands into his eyes to relieve some pressure. "I feel like the next morning. Are you sure Leigh's going to be okay?"

"She'll be fine when she wakes up. She'll probably feel like she's had a great night's sleep. You took all the damage upon yourself and held on to it. There is more to healing another person than just drawing in their injuries. You have to bring it in, fix it, and let it back out again. If it was anyone but you, you'd probably be a vegetable now. Fortunately, your thick skull seems to have an easier time dealing with psychic trauma than most."

"I saw something, inside her head, and I don't know what to do about it." Terry fidgeted with his hands. "How much do you know about what happened to her?"

David shrugged. "Blue Eye Burn out is what I heard."

Terry shook his head, "No. I've seen blue eye burnout." He dropped his eyes to the ground and his voice took on a dark tone. "There isn't anything left of them. I mean, at all, David. Nothing but ash and memories."

"You're wrong, Terry." David said. He turned away and leaned on the iron railing, looking out over the town. "It doesn't always happen that

74

way. You've seen it take magi in the Orders, right? Have you ever seen what it does to one of us mere mortals?"

"I guess not." Terry lit another cigarette and took a drag. "David, you know brains, right?"

"I guess." He turned back around. "I've helped some people with some problems. I've even been known to give advice to a wayward mage, from time to time."

"Have you ever seen someone wall off a part of their memory? Just completely cut out a part of their mind?"

"Sure." David nodded. "We all do. It's how humans cope with memories and experiences that are too painful. You can't remember everything that ever happens to you. It'd drive you completely insane."

"Have you seen someone do it on purpose?"

David's brow furrowed. After a long pause, he sighed and nodded. "Yeah, I've seen it."

"I think Leigh did that, David. I think she figured out how to do something big, and it scared her. Scared her enough that she didn't just force herself to forget out how to do it, but forced herself to forget how to figure it out." He thought about the symbols etched into the stone walls. "And she showed it to me. I don't know what it means, but Soulbinder recognized it." He took another drag from the cigarette. "And I need to forget it."

"Why?" David asked. "You just said you didn't know what it means. Why would you need to forget?"

"I couldn't understand the symbols. The patterns were too small and complex for me to figure them out. I didn't have enough time to put them together, and I'm not that smart, even if I could."

"Sounds like there isn't a problem."

"Munindwade won't have those restrictions. He'll remember the patterns perfectly. He'll be able to figure them out. Sooner or later, he'll know. I have to forget them... and I have to do it before the next time I touch him."

"You're afraid if he figures it out he'll use it?"

"No." Terry said quietly. His other thoughts went unsaid.

"So you want me to remove it from your head. Is that what you're asking?" David stared at him with cold blue eyes. Terry nodded without looking up to meet his gaze. "Well, in that case. No."

"No?" The perpetual anger started to rear up inside him and Terry felt his nails dig into his palms as his knuckles clenched. His words came out in sharp, clipped grunts. "What do you mean 'no'? If Soulbinder is right, what I know is the magical equivalent of a nuclear bomb."

"Well, now that you put it that way," David said. "Fuck no."

"Why the hell not?" Terry's voice boomed. He stopped and took a deep breath, burying the anger back down inside of him. "Give me one good reason."

"Because, Terry. Playing around inside someone's mind is dangerous. Because, even if I was willing to do it with someone else, which I'm not, I still wouldn't risk it with you. The last time I was deep in your

76

head, there were." He paused and pointed at Terry's chest. "Unforeseen side-effects."

"He will never forget it, you realize that, right? That information will exist for all of eternity." Terry said.

The door opened while he was talking, and Terry held up the pack of cigarettes for Gabriel. Leigh took them instead, pulled one out, and lit it.

"It doesn't matter if he remembers." She took a drag off the cigarette and let the plume of smoke hang in the air. Her mannerisms had changed. She stood straighter, carried herself with more confidence. She gestured with the cigarette in a way that seemed practiced, but that Terry had never seen before. "How's the saying go? The avalanche has already started. It's too late for the pebbles to vote?"

CHAPTER 14

Leigh sat the intricately carved wooden box on the table and ran her fingers in precise practiced movements across the different panels. "I'll tell you about the stones, but there are some things you need to know first." There was a click and one of the panels popped down. The lid of the box cracked open and she pulled a wooden globe from inside. "Yes, I remember you. Yes, I remember the last five years, as well as anyone else remembers them, at least. Yes, I am still the same person, more or less."

She thumbed the globe, causing the shifting lines on the surface to glow softly for a few seconds before fading back into a dull scratch. She held it in the palm of one had, grinning at a fond memory. "I wanted to make miracles."

Terry sat opposite her, watching her speak. He could see the subtle changes in the way she moved, the way she spoke. Even her face seemed as if someone had adjusted the focus on an image and brought it to a sharper, cleaner resolution. A clarity that he hadn't even noticed was missing before. The entire sense of her presence seemed more grounded, less airy. Her emotions were calmer, deeper. She just radiated a sense of being more than she had before.

"Go on," Gabriel prompted. He was leaning forward with his hands stretched flat across the table. His eyes shone with a warm light, and Terry knew he was doing his best to not just wrap his arms around her in a hug. Gabriel had known her longer than any of the rest of them. He had known her before the war, before she'd become the woman Terry had known for the last few years. The look on his face told them everything. His friend was back from the dead. He smiled as he slipped into his preacher voice. "We're listening, and we're not judging."

Leigh looked up at Terry and caught his eye. There was a new pain there, one that she hadn't had that morning. "You know what the war was like. It was chaos. Everyone was looking for an edge. Something that made them a little bit faster, a little bit stronger." She dropped her eyes to the table. "A little bit richer." She reached across and took Terry's pack of cigarettes from where they lay on the table. She pulled one out, grabbed a small red stone from the rack on the wall, and lit it. "I didn't start out that way. I want you to know that."

He nodded and pulled out his own cigarette. "None of us did. It was a war. It changes everyone."

She took a long drag on the cigarette, flicked the ash into the open box, and blew the smoke out through her nose. "Most of the women in my family are Vedma, going back generations. Some of my aunts weren't really into it, but my mother and grandmother were very deeply involved in the practices. It wasn't just a career for them. They believed in the religion, through and through."

David held up his hand, drawing everyone's attention. "Sorry. Vedma?"

Before Terry could start a lecture, Gabriel leaned forward. "Wise women. Slavic Witches. Not too different from Hecites or a Druid. And that is more than enough explanation for this conversation."

Terry sighed and rolled his eyes. Leigh just nodded.

"Close enough, anyway," she said. "The Mennonites near where I lived called us Hedge witches. We'd make medicines and charms for them, and in exchange, they'd help us build barns and grow pot. You know, the usual stuff." She reached under her shirt and pulled out a small clay disk etched with a single rune. "So I grew up making whatever toys I wanted to make. I had a knack. This was the first thing I'd ever made. It's just a simple charm. It glows if you concentrate hard enough. Hell, I've sold hundreds of them."

She fiddled with the charm, her eyes distant. Terry felt a flood of nostalgia wash off of her and saw David tense from the corner of his eye. She tapped out the ash from her cigarette and huffed a little sigh. "My entire life, I've had a gift. I could figure out how to make things work. I could just kind of see it in my head. The problem was that I didn't have the oomph." She held her hand up to examine her nails, and then clicked them down on the table. "I felt like a kid playing baseball. I knew how the mechanics of it all worked, but my arms weren't strong enough to knock it out of the park."

Terry took a deep breath. "And Blue Eye was your solution."

"Yes," she said quietly. "But not the way you think. I could see how to make myself stronger, and I did. I made a magical steroid to make me the Mark McGuire of magic." She snuffed the cigarette. "I didn't intend to let it out, but, there were others that needed it. People I trusted that just wanted to up their game."

Terry let it sink in, his own memories of the glowing blue liquid streaming into his mind. He'd thought he'd forgotten them, pushed them away. There they were. So many young mages had taken the drug, given themselves a boost to live a little longer. He remembered when it had changed. The need to be a little better had been replaced with the need to keep going. His skin crawled with the memory and he shook his head to force it back down.

"So how'd it happen?" He tried to keep the accusation out of his voice.

Leigh clenched her fist, popping her knuckles. "I met a boy." She sighed and leaned back in the chair. "He was beautiful, the kind of man-pretty that you see in Gap commercials." She sighed. "He was an order mage, a front line soldier with the Forge. He was constantly afraid for his life. At first, I just made it for him, but eventually, I showed him how to do it himself."

"And once one of us had it, the rest of us had to have it, too," Terry said absently. His voice was distant and weak. "It spread like wildfire."

Leigh's eyes were downcast as she nodded, "Once everyone was hooked, things started to snowball. I had all the hopes and dreams, but artifice isn't cheap. I needed to fund the projects. I," she paused, regret spilling into her voice. "I let myself get pulled into a lifestyle. I made a choice. I made deals." Her eyes met Gabriel's and dropped back to the table.

"I remember," Gabriel said quietly. "I remember you coming to us and asking for help. You wanted out." It was his turn to drop his eyes to the table. "And we couldn't help you. Something happened, though. The next time I saw you after that, you had changed."

Leigh nodded again. "Lydia." She leaned back in her chair and pinched the bridge of her nose. "Lydia was a smart kid in a real bad place. She was my Chad." She looked up at Terry, her eyes carrying an extra weight. "She was my right hand and my pet project rolled into one. I met her at a party she shouldn't have been at. She was fifteen or sixteen, I was never really sure, but she was smart. You know how we all have one of those friends that make us feel like a moron? She would have made that person seem like a gibbering idiot. She was the one that made everything work. She was the one that figured everything out. I made the product and she turned it into an Empire. I thought I was saving her."

"Something happened to her?" David asked. He reached out and squeezed Leigh hand, trying to reassure her.

"She died. That's what happened." She squeezed David's hand back and pushed herself up from the table. "Long story short, a deal went bad. It was my fault. I couldn't deal with it, so I got rid of it. I did what I thought I had to do, and erased that part of my life. That's when I stumbled back to the temple and Gabe took me in."

Terry hesitated, not sure exactly what to say. "Where do the stones come in?" He blurted out.

"I told you, I'm not strong enough to do what I wanted to do. Even on Blue Eye, I wasn't strong enough to keep things running, so I found a power supply."

Terry nodded. "That's why you have the Leyfon. You charged the stones with pulses from ley lines. That's how you charged the shield stone."

"No, the ley lines were part of creating the stones, but it's much worse than that. I took a lesson from Midnight and got the power I needed the same way they do."

A sad realization tore its way through Terry's mind. He let his own eyes fall to the table and tried not to let tears well up in his eyes. "They're spirit prisons."

"Yes." She picked up the pack of cigarettes and took another. She lit it and took a deep drag. "Spirits, especially old ones, are powerful. The stones I made, the ones you keep finding, they were powered by spirits ready to fade. I convinced them to fuel the stones instead. It seemed like a perfect solution."

"So, what did you do with them? When you decided to give up that life?" Terry asked.

"I put everything in storage. I paid a couple of years up front. It probably got auctioned off a year or more ago. I kept one chest, you know, in case of an emergency, and some trinkets to sell off here and there."

"So," Terry said. "We're back to square one. We have no idea who bought the stones or what they're using them for."

Leigh shook her head. "We know they've figured out how to make new ones. They're replacing the ones they're using up. That's why they're broken. The spirits inside are burned out or faded off. They're changing the batteries in whatever they've built. But," she fiddled with the broken blue stone lying on the table. "They're not very good at it. Otherwise, they'd have recharged these."

"We also know something else," Gabriel said, grinning. "We know what storage place Leigh used, right." He waited while she nodded. "Storage places have to keep records, pay taxes, stuff like that." He looked over at Terry. "If there are records of who bought the locker, we know who's using the stones."

Terry pushed himself up from the table and pulled out his cellphone. "I'll call Slate and see if he can get ahold of those records." He pushed the rest of the pack of cigarettes across the table to Leigh. "Thank you. We've got a lead now, and I'm going to nail this mother-fucker."

Leigh smiled. "Let me know how I can help."

"For now, we wait for Slate to do his thing." He looked around the table. "I've got a phone call to make."

CHAPTER 15

Terry pushed open the door to his apartment, cellphone pressed to one ear. "Sounds like you've got this covered." He tossed the keys onto the table by the door and stepped across the torn masking tape on the hardwood floor. Munindwade scurried in behind him, carrying a stack of mail bundled in his arms. "Paper work is all yours," he said into the phone.

"Thanks," Slate answered. "I appreciate the importance of my role. I'm glad I can be of valuable service. Thank you for keeping me in the loop."

"Oh, come on, Jared. This stuff's important, too. You know that. It's what we've got. I promise, when a monster shows up for us to fight, I'll give you a call."

"Meh, I'm no stranger to leg work, Terry. Trust me. This job is rarely monster-slaying and duels-to-the-death."

"Not for you," Terry said, lowering himself into the old recliner. "Some of us actually have interesting lives." He pulled the handle and kicked his up his feet. "I'll see you in the morning."

"Yeah, yeah. I'll be here. Good night, Terry. Try to stay out of trouble for one evening."

"I'm beat, Slate. I'm going to crawl into bed as soon as I get off the phone. So, good night." He tapped the end button before Slate could reply. He moved to sit the phone on the ledge behind his head, but it started buzzing almost immediately. Terry looked down at the screen, and then quickly answered the phone. "Mitchell? What's up? It's almost midnight."

"Terry?" A ragged voice asked. "I need your help. She's throwing a fit and I don't know what to do!" His voice cracked at the end and Terry recognized the exasperation. Mitchell was a good father, a great father, but he was not, in any way, prepared to deal with a four-year-old throwing around the magical mojo of a person ten times her age.

"Do you have the Dora DVDs?" Terry asked. "The ones I left there?"

"Yeah," Mitchel answered with a skeptical voice.

"Okay, put them on. I'll be there in a bit."

"Terry," Mitchell said. "Thank you."

"I'll see you in a half-hour. Survive and thank me then."

Terry tapped the end button again and stuffed the phone back into his pocket. He groaned as he pushed the footrest back down on the chair and dragged himself to his feet. Munindwade jumped down from the bed and scurried over to him. "We're not going out again, are we? When was the last time you slept? Humans need sleep."

"I'm not tired," Terry lied. "Sara's giving Mitchell problems again. She can't help it, but he can't help her either. She needs me, so I go." He stumbled through the dark room to the door. "Come on."

86

He opened the door and waited while Munindwade hurried out. He took a long look at the room and the realization hit him as to how empty the apartment seemed with just one person living in it. "We should get a cat," he said as he closed the door behind him.

"No, a dog!" Munindwade chimed. He climbed the stairs and waited at the landing for Terry to catch up. "A furry terrier. I could call him Sir Rupert and ride him into battle."

"I don't know that I like the idea of being known as Terry, the guy who owns the terrier." He pushed the door to the front landing open and nodded at the pair of college kids sitting on the stoop smoking a cigarette. His new neighbors were an annoyance, but he'd managed to ignore them so far. The fog that wafting out of their apartment at all hours of the day made him wonder why they'd bothered to come outside to smoke. He'd never bothered to ask them.

Terry ignored them as he walked down the sidewalk to his car parked along the street. He'd learned his lesson about getting involved with his neighbors. These kids could do whatever they wanted. It wasn't his job to teach them right from wrong. He'd opened the passenger door and let Munindwade scuttle into the car and was about to climb in the driver's side when one of the kids came walking over.

"Hey, man," he asked with a slurred voice, "You or your leprechaun holding?"

Terry sighed. He reached into his jacket and started working to pull something out of his pocket. The other one came up to the car, a gleam of hope in his eyes. Terry raised his chin in greeting and produced the leather wallet. He sat it down on the roof of his car and pushed it across to the two kids. The first one picked it up, stared at the brass badge hanging inside, then handed it to his friend.

His friend held it up so he could read it in the street light and then looked at Terry with wide eyes. "You're a cop?"

Terry shrugged. "Not exactly." He held out his hand and the kid passed the badge back over to him. "I work for the Secret Service. Have either of you fine young gentlemen ever had thoughts of overthrowing your government."

"What?' the first kid asked.

"Have either of you ever thought to yourself, 'Man, we should all just live in love and anarchy, man.'" Terry stuffed the badge back into his pocket. "Because, like, dude, that might be treason, man."

"Whatever," the second kid said. He grabbed his friend by the elbow and pulled him back to the stoop. "You could've just said no, man."

Terry climbed into the car and started the engine. "I've got to find a new place," he told Munindwade. "I'm getting too old for this shit."

Munindwade stood in the passenger seat, watching the two teenagers on the stoop. He turned back to Terry with one eyebrow raised. "You're twenty-one," he chided.

"Yeah, well." Terry put the car in drive and pulled away from the curb. "You're ugly."

CHAPTER 16

Terry parked in the first space he could find and let Munindwade ride on his shoulders as he crossed the lot to Mitchell's building. He stopped inside the first set of doors and pushed the button on the intercom. "Hey, it's me," he said, and waited for the door to pop open.

The speaker squawked and Mitchell's disembodied voice cracked as he came on. "Thank god, it's about time." The door beeped a moment later.

Terry pushed it open and crossed to the elevators on the other side of the lobby. He waved at the security guard sitting behind the glass window to one side. The heavy-set older man, nodded in greeting, causing the tufts of curly gray hair to bounce at the corners of a shiny balding head. He idly flipped the pages of his magazine and went back to staring at the monitors.

The elevator opened, and Terry retreated inside, quickly tapping the button for the fifth floor. "I think that guy hates me," he muttered as the doors slid shut.

"Nah," Munindwade assured him. "He just didn't want you to know that he's reading 'Juggs' magazine."

Terry was still snickering when the doors opened again. He could hear the roar of an angry child fuming from down the hall and he grimaced as he stepped out. "You know what I can't believe?" he asked the homunculus.

"That people still buy porn in magazine form?"

"Well, yeah." Terry stopped outside the door to Mitchell's apartment. "But also that we're still doing all of this. Doesn't it feel like we've just been going in circles?" He knocked on the door, and Mitchell immediately threw it open. He leaned out into the hall and looked to either side with wild, manic eyes. His fluffy red hair was standing on end, and sweat was pouring down his face.

"Did you come alone? Tell me you brought some backup!"

Terry pushed him gently back into the apartment and surveyed the damage. Toys were scattered across the floor in piles that formed a maze of toddler debris that threatened to come crashing down. He stopped and gave Mitchell a look of sympathy.

"Sara?" He said in a bit of a sing song voice. "What are you doing?" A giggle from somewhere in the living room was the only response. He turned back to Mitchell. "You look like you could use some sleep."

"Am I a horrible father, Terry? I can't even get my little girl to lie down! She's." he waived his hands in a frantic circle. "She's going insane!"

"You are an awesome father," Terry told him. "Go lay down, Mitchell. The Calvary's here. She's just coming into her own. What you have here is a child hopped up on super sugar. I'm officially relieving you of duty."

"Dora didn't work, Terry. Dora didn't work." Mitchell rubbed at his head. "She's never been like this before. I don't know what to do."

"Yes you do," Terry reassured him. "But it takes a village, right? Besides, Munindwade wanted to come see her anyway." He shooed Mitchell to the back of the apartment and stalked into the mess of a living room. "Sarah," he drawled out. "Where are you, goblin?"

A giggle came from his left, and he turned pointedly to his right and began to pick up the toys on the floor and tossing them into the empty toy box. "Maybe she's gone missing," he said to Munindwade. "We'll just have to get a new goblin. Can't let mommy and daddy go goblin-less."

A sudden crash came from next to Munindwade and the homunculus went scurrying across the room followed by a flash of bright red hair. "Randy!" Sara screamed as she snatched the homunculus up off the ground.

Terry spun around and grabbed her in the same way, lifting her in the air in fit of giggles. She squeezed Munindwade to her chest and Terry put one finger against his lips. "Shh! Daddy's sleeping," he whispered and winked at her. "How about we clean up this room so when he wakes up he'll be super happy?"

She shook her head. "Nooooo," she bubbled out. "Dora!"

"I don't know," he swung her over his shoulder and let her dangle down his back. "You think you deserve Dora?"

91

"Yes!" Terry felt Munindwade thump against the back of his ankles as tiny hands started trying to crawl down the backs of his legs. "Come back, Randy!"

He pulled her back up and held her in the air over his head. "Okay, Goblin, tell me what you've been doing." She just shook her head and smiled coyly at him. He bounced her once into the air, then turned and tossed her onto the couch with a thump and an explosion of laughter.

"Okay, then." He turned away from her and began gathering toys from the floor again. "I guess I'll just clean all this up on my own, and then, maybe, we'll watch some Dora."

Sara stood up on the couch and crossed her arms. She stomped one foot with a humff and jumped down to chase after Munindwade again. This time he saw her coming and ducked beneath the coffee table with a squeal. Sara dropped to her hands and knees and stuck her head down against the floor to watch him.

"Come out, Randy!" She commanded and a flood of authority echoed out of her voice and bounced across the floor in a wave that crumpled against the homunculus. He crawled to the far end of the table and stuck out his tongue at her.

Terry turned back around to watch the little girl. Steam rolled off of her as she forced power out into the air with no control. It was the sloppy, unfocused will of raw talent released without the skill to control it. He recognized what she was doing and squatted down beside her, putting one hand on her back. "Sara," he said with a sharp voice. "Stop."

92

"Why?" She whined.

He waved a hand to push away the torrent of power she threw at him and gave her a dark look. "You're being very mean right now."

She sat back in shock. He'd done two things she'd never seen him do before, not to her. He'd snapped at her and he'd told her she was being bad. Mean was a concept she understood. The cartoons told her what mean was. They told her that mean was bad. Tears started to wash up in her eyes and her cheeks turned red. "I didn't want to be mean," she sobbed.

Terry pulled her into a hug. "I know goblin. You didn't mean it. It's okay, but now you know, right." She nodded against his chest. "So you won't do it again?" She nodded again. He held her, rubbing her back and drawing the energy out of her. After a bit, she yawned, and he picked her up and moved to the rocking chair. It had been a long time since he'd rocked her to sleep, and it was comforting to do it again. He drew the excess power out of her as she drifted off to sleep, and kept rocking her for an hour after she'd passed out. It was a test of will for him to finally carry her to bed.

He closed the door to her room, making sure the moon on her wall was glowing softly before he returned to the living room. He took in the mess again, sighed, and began to stack the toys back into the toy box.

"You don't have to clean," Munindwade said, carrying his own armful of stuffed animals to the plastic bin. "Mitchell will still let you come over and see her."

Terry shrugged. "It's not about that right now. I want to help. They're family." He gathered up the leftover dishes and ran a sink full of hot water. "Mitchell is a great guy. He loves his daughter and he'd do anything for her, but he just doesn't have the skills to handle a kid like her. He needs help. I help out, and he lets me play uncle. It works." He turned away from the sink to find Munindwade staring at him, hands on his hips and mouth agape. "What?"

"Nothing," Munindwade said. "I'm just surprised."

"Surprised I'm willing to help Mitchell out? I thought that's what we did?"

"No," Munindwade said. "I'm surprised you're okay with how it all worked out. You were so mad at Carrie for not letting you see her."

Terry shrugged and went back to scrubbing dishes. "I don't know. I guess I just decided that keeping my promises to Sara were more important than spiting her bitch mom." He stacked the last of the clean dishes into the strainer, wiped the cabinets down and moved over to the couch with a yawn.

"That's very mature of you," Munindwade said, climbing up to sit on the back of the couch as Terry lay down and kicked off his shoes.

"Nope," Terry said as he stuffed one of the couch pillows under his head. "I'm still a jerk. Part of me is plenty happy enough to admit that this means I'm winning the break up."

Munindwade snorted out a laugh, but Terry just waved him away and let himself fall asleep.

CHAPTER 17

Terry pushed the door to his office open to find it already crowded. Chad had taken up residency at his desk and was busy chatting with someone on the phone. He had Terry's laptop open to a rare books website and was taking notes from whoever he was talking to. Gabriel was sitting in the folding chair, thumbing through a pile of loose papers. "What are you guys doing here ass-early?"

"Slate called me this morning, so I hooked a ride over with the kid," Gabriel said. He held up the stack of papers. "Looks like we've got most of the records for the last couple of years back from the storage place. We should have more this afternoon. Ironically, they're stored off site."

Terry stepped into the office and gestured for Chad to get out of his chair with one hand. The teenager stood up and awkwardly walked around to the far side of the desk, phone pressed between his shoulder and ear, still making notes on the notepad. "Yeah, hand-written recreation," he said into the phone. "Probably from the 1920s or so." He paused, rolling his eyes at whatever was being said on the other end. "No, I don't have any pictures, but I can get them."

"What's he up to?" Terry asked Gabriel. He fiddled with the stuff on his desk, putting everything back into place. Munindwade climbed up from his bag on the floor and sat down on the wooden box to peer at the laptop screen. His fingers twitched a little as he drooled at the store's inventory.

"We thought we'd put the kid to work. If he's not going to school, he might as well earn what you pay him. There have been a lot of old order books turning up in the community lately. Sue's got him hunting down the best price he can get for them. One at a time."

"Yes, I have your email. Yes," Chad was almost shouting into the phone. He made a spinning motion with his hand. "Thanks, yeah. I'll email you pictures this afternoon." He placed the phone back on the base and huffed out a deep breath. "Christ, these guys!"

"How many books do you have to pawn off?" Terry asked. He pulled his laptop back from Munindwade before the homunculus started typing in his debit card number on the site.

"Almost two hundred," Gabriel said. He broke the stack of records in half and handed it across to Terry. "So far, he hasn't sold any."

"It's not my fault," Chad protested, his voice cracking a little. "These book guys, man they don't want to buy anything without seeing every crack and crevice. One of them asked me if I'd had the paper acid tested! I don't even know what the fuck that means."

"Language," Terry said without looking up. "Hey, Gabriel, are these the originals?"

Gabriel shrugged. "I have no idea. Why?"

96

"Because I need some photocopies. Chad, you want to run an errand for me?" Terry started bundling the pages back into a stack, secured with rubber bands. "Take these down to Kinko's and have copies made. The entire stack Chad and don't miss a single page."

"Can't I just use the photocopier down the hall?" Chad whined. "The Kinko's smells like rank ass. It's almost as bad as the gaming store."

"The office copier jams up every time someone runs double-sided," Terry told him. He pulled out his wallet and gave the kid a couple of twenties. "That should cover it, but if it doesn't, call me. Actually, if it does, call me anyway. I might have some other errands for you to run before you get back."

"Yes, sir," Chad huffed. He grabbed his keys from Terry's desk and headed for the door.

"Two copies, Chad!" Terry called down the hall after him. "Double-sided. Black and white!"

Terry slumped down in the chair and started going through his desk. "I need more bitch work for him to do," he muttered to himself.

"Why?" Gabriel asked. "Why not just, I don't know, command him to go to school."

Terry shrugged. "If someone had commanded me to go to school when I was sixteen, I would've told them to eat my dick. If I make him do more bitch work than school ever dreamed of, he'll beg to be let back in."

"Your logic is astounding and flawless."

"Hey, Terry," Munindwade said from the corner of the desk. "You've got lots of emails from Slate."

Terry looked up to find the homunculus had taken the computer and had already managed to open about fifty tabs on the browser. "Looks like files from the storage place."

Terry grumbled. "We have digital copies?" He asked Gabriel. "Why didn't you tell me that before I sent the kid out to waste money?"

"You didn't ask," Gabriel said defensively. "Besides, I don't know why you wanted copies anyway. We could have split the stack and worked just as fast."

Terry shook his head. "No, we couldn't." He opened the email and pulled up a folder on the network drive. It contained a couple of hundred PDF files. "Muni, how fast can you read these?" Munindwade sat down at the laptop and started popping the files open one-by-one.

"Uh," he said. "Twenty minutes?"

"Okay." Terry stood up from the table and pulled the pack of cigarettes from his pocket. "You do that, figure out who bought Leigh's locker, and Gabriel and I will be out on the stairs."

"Can I buy a book afterwards?" Munindwade asked, already popping through the files.

"If it cost less than $5, sure. Knock yourself out." Terry stepped out into the hall, Gabriel following. He closed the door and headed down the hall past Slate's office to the emergency door that led to a concrete platform and little ramp outside. He reached up and pulled the cord free from the alarm and pushed the door open.

The fire alarm went off. Slate stepped out of his office, to see Terry standing in the open door. "I thought I showed you how to deactivate the emergency alarm."

"I did!" Terry protested, holding the loose cord in his hand. He started to say something else, but the smell of burning plastic came wafting down the hall from the direction of the gym and labs. There was a loud rumble and the building shook around them.

"Was that a bomb?" Gabriel asked.

"Not exactly," Terry said as the explosive waves of magical heat washed past them. Slate gave him a nod and he started jogging down the hall, jerking the key from around his neck as he ran. Behind him, he heard the agent barking orders for Gabriel and Munindwade to evacuate with everyone else.

A thick black smoke ran over the ceiling, pouring through the door leading to the gym he'd been sparring in just a few days before. He held out a hand to the door, feeling the warmth radiate up from it.

"What is it?" Slate asked. He had his pistol out and ready, but it was the medallion he wore around his chest that Terry noticed. The little ward was a powerful one, a symbol of protection for those that uphold justice. Most small enchantments would slide right past it and more than a few large ones would be reduced to nearly harmless by its shield. He wasn't sure how well it would hold up to prolonged exposure.

"Spirit fire... It's not real until it is," Terry said, and when Slate gave him a dirty look, he rolled his eyes. "You feel the heat, but there's no flame. When it gets hot enough, though, stuff might just burst into flames anyway."

"I don't understand the difference," Slate said. "That's good enough for all practical purposes."

Terry held the key out to his side, letting the sword's weight fall into his hand. "Real fire is a helluva lot harder to control." Terry put a hand on the door, and looked over his shoulder with Slate. "You ready?"

Slate nodded, Terry pulled open the door, and they both darted into the furnace.

CHAPTER 18

A thick red haze hung in the air, blurring the shapes that moved in the center of the gym. Long, thin bodies with short rear legs and stumpy arms swam through the heat, circling the large bulk of Roderick's construct at the center of the gym. They moved in chaotic swirls, gliding over the floor with an asymmetric grace. The construct turned in a slow circle, tracking the movements of the flames.

One of the forms darted forward in a torrent of fire. It slammed into the construct sending a hiss of steam boiling into the air. A section of the construct's body dulled briefly before a bubbling noise brought back that shine. Terry recognized the technique and cursed himself for not grabbing a bottle of water from the fridge in his office.

"Salamanders," Slate hissed from behind him. "I hate salamanders." He raised the pistol and began tracking their movements.

"Yeah," Terry said. He stepped back to move from between Slate's gun and the elementals. "But, why are they here?"

"Looks to me like they've got a problem with Frankenstein over there." Slate nodded toward the construct.

"Frankenstein was the scientist." Terry darted his eyes across the gym, looking for any other signs of movement. "So, where is Frankenstein? I don't see Max anywhere."

The construct made a sudden, low rumbling noise and darted out with one huge hand. The fist wrapped around one of the twisting forms, jerking it from the ground. It grabbed the lower half of the body with its other hand and began to pull, stretching the elemental across its chest. A scream like steam from a kettle magnified by stadium amplifiers accompanying a pair of giant claws on a chalkboard erupted from the creature as the flesh of its body gave way under the stress. Thick pools of flaming ichor plopped from the two halves of its body.

"Shit," Terry muttered under his breath. "We've got to move. Now!" He sprinted into the gym, slashing out with the black sword. One of the forms slid in his way, its body a cascade of burning membrane. It swung out with its flat tail and Terry had to leap into the air at the last second.

Thunder roared from behind him and the creature's flaming blood splattered across the floor. Terry landed just past the growing flames and shot Slate a dirty look. "You don't want to do that," he shouted back at the agent. "You don't want to fuck with the little ones."

Another scream came from the middle of the room as the construct smashed one against the floor with bone-shattering force. Flames erupted from its blood, spreading in either direction in long, deep arcs. Terry darted for the edge of one line, driving the blade down into the line to stop it from touching.

The blade crashed against the wall of fire in a shower of sparks. Terry stumbled backward as the flames rose to the ceiling in a geyser. The remaining salamanders all dove into the circle, bodies sloshing away as they rejoined the flames.

"Too late," Terry said as he took a few steps away from the gate.

"What just happened?" Slate asked. "I've seen salamanders before and they didn't do that."

"They opened a gate," Terry said quietly. "We've got a problem." The flames rose up one more time, sending thick clouds of black smoke sliding over the inside of the roof. The ceiling started to catch, sending tendrils of flame licking down the walls.

Flames flared up along the circle, burning brightly for only a heartbeat before collapsing to reveal the massive body of a giant red bullfrog. Its head brushed the top of the gym and its massive golden eyes narrowed on them. It began to laugh as it pushed itself forward on hands large enough to hold a man. It sniffed at the air and focused on Terry.

"I smell parasite," it said. Smoke rolled out through its nostrils and mouth as it spoke. "I smell the tick that murdered that hag."

Terry stumbled backward and covered his eyes as the heat of the breath washed over him. He hadn't been ready for the juvenile salamanders. There was no way he could fight one that was fully grown. He shielded his face with his left arm and readied the sword in his right. He knew he'd only get one shot at this.

"No excuses, little tick?" the bullfrog asked. "Do you deny that you feasted on her? Turned her into a slave for your own power?"

Terry felt Slate dragging him back and let himself be pulled toward the door. "This place is going up, where the hell are the sprinklers?" Slate grunted as he hauled Terry back. The amulet on his chest flared with a strong white light, but even through his clothes Terry was beginning to feel it heating up.

He pulled himself free from the agent's arms and forced himself to stare at the elemental without blinking, without flinching. "You think you can fight me?" he asked, "You think I killed Saddy, and you still think you can win?"

"Yes," the bullfrog croaked.

"Try me." Terry reached into himself and pulled on the well of power he'd gained from Saddy. He wrapped the cool, damp strength around himself and charged forward, Soulbinder at his side. The bullfrog leaned back; its chest puffed out, and then spat. The glob of molten phlegm went sailing through the air. Terry struck out with the blade, slicing it in half.

The phlegm shattered into red mist that began funneling down the sword, pouring into Terry's arm. The heat caused the blade to warp and bend and the skin on his right hand began to blister. He screamed as his instincts pushed the cool energy down into his wrist. Something gave.

His right hand went numb and the sword vanished, leaving the end of the black key jutting out between the fingers locked in pain. He tried to scream, but the smoke had begun filling his lungs and he could only cough and choke.

"So much for your borrowed power," the elemental roared as it towered over him. "I thought Saddy would have been better. Maybe I should have taken her a long time ago."

The construct sprung into Terry's vision. Its hulking body lumbering forward, one hand extended. Something happened, an impact crashed over the room, and for a moment, Terry could swear he saw the creation's left hand at the center of a massive red vortex.

The elemental roared and a ring of flames wrapped around it again, this time sending it back to the other side of the veil. Terry watched from the floor, barely able to breath. Roderick's construct turned from the circle and bent down, scooped him up, and carried him from the flaming building.

Terry barely had time to notice the red stone drop out of it before he passed out.

CHAPTER 19

Terry awoke with his wrists strapped down at his sides. Panic immediately crashed into his mind. He thrashed wildly against the bonds until pain clenched the muscles in his arms.

"Easy, easy," a calm, gravelly voice whispered in his ear.

"Your skin is tender. Don't tear it open again."

Stanley's liver-spotted hand came down to rest against his forearm, and Terry relaxed. The last couple of years had not been kind to his mentor. Stanley White had managed to put off aging for the last century or so, but time was definitely catching up to him. His face crinkled loosely at the corners of dim eyes as he smiled at his former pupil through stringy silver hair.

"Where am I?" Terry asked. His head was swimming through a fog of sedatives, but he could tell he was in a hospital room of some kind. The sterile white walls and sheets gleamed with the light streaming in through the blinds. The bed to his left was currently unoccupied. The muted TV hanging in the corner was tuned to a twenty-four hour news channel hosted by an anchor that, the closed captioning assured Terry, was "passionately crying."

"You're at the Trauma Center. You burned yourself pretty bad. Channeling fire, Terry? I taught you better than that." Stanley lowered himself back into the chair with the speed of a particularly slow glacier. "The human body can't handle fire unassisted. It'll burn you from the inside. If you weren't the key bearer, you'd be dead already."

"Where's Munindwade?" The fear of losing the homunculus rang sharper in his voice than he had realized before. "If something happened to him..."

"I gave it some cash and sent it to the cafeteria a few minutes ago." Terry caught Stanley watching his eyes and raised his eyebrows in response.

"What?"

"We couldn't get it to leave the room without a direct order," Stanley said slowly. "It sure is loyal."

"Yeah, he's pretty stubborn, too. I hope you didn't give him too much money. He's a walking computer with a sweet tooth. You'll get whatever pennies you have left over after he finagles every possible cupcake or donut he can."

"There it is," Stanley said, leaning back in the chair. "I thought something had changed."

Terry stared at him in confusion. "What?"

"When did it become a 'he'?" Stanley asked. "I thought you were adamant that it had no gender."

Terry shrugged as best he could with his wrists bound. "Well, he made a pretty convincing argument. He said it was pretty insensitive of me to recognize Suez's gender choices but not his. Also, he threatened to build his own penis out of clay, and I thought that could get awkward fast."

Stanley nodded. "Well, at least you're growing up in one way or another." He leaned forward again in the chair and rested his arms along the bar holding Terry's arms down. "Want to tell me what happened with Saddy?"

Terry turned his head away and looked down at the IV in his arm. "No," he mumbled, but turned back to his mentor. "But I'm guessing I'm not getting out of this bed until I do."

"Your intuition is growing strong," Stanley said in a flat tone, and then a breath later began chuckling. "Tell me what happened. I'm not here to judge you. Yet."

Terry told him everything. He explained about the empty sylph prison, Saddy's death, Leigh's involvement and finally his encounter with the Salamander. "And that's that. It was Tiny. Roderick's damn construct is powered by the stones, and it's over now. He got the fourth stone. Now, I just turn him over to Slate and go on to the next job."

There was a quiet thump at the door and a second later the handle clicked open. Munindwade hung to it by one hand and dragged a bag of pastries with his other. His eyes exploded open as he swung into the room, excitement rushing into them with the recognition that Terry was awake. "You lived," he squawked as he dropped to the floor and scurried over to the bed, still dragging the pastries behind him. He climbed up onto the bed and pulled a Danish from the bag. "Here, I got you something!" He placed the Danish on Terry's chest and retreated with the remaining confections to the foot of the bed.

Stanley watched the display and shook his head. "I'm afraid Jared won't be arresting anyone any time soon," he said with a hint of sadness in his voice.

"Why not?" Terry asked.

"He hasn't committed a crime by US Law. This is outside the Secret Service's jurisdiction. They have no authority here." Stanley let the words hang heavy in the air, his wrinkled face hardening into stone. "You have to deal with him."

Munindwade paused, a large cruller halfway to his mouth and stared at Terry with wide eyes. "You can't, Terry," he said quietly. "You can't do that. It's against the rules."

"Don't read my thoughts, Muni, it's creepy." Terry looked away from the horrified homunculus. "What do I need to do?"

Stanley shrugged. "Make a decision." He clicked his mouth shut and leaned back in the chair to watch Terry's thoughts play out on his face.

Pain and anger swirled around inside Terry's head. It was a dizzy uncomfortable feeling made even stronger by the morphine pumping into his arms. He looked down at Munindwade waiting at his feet. The expression on Munindwade's face told Terry that the homunculus wanted him to say he'd find a way to deal with the crime that didn't involve murder.

He wanted to find one himself, but he couldn't see anything. The laws of one government didn't supersede the laws of the Order. He had to fulfill his oath to Saddy. There was no choice there.

"Untie me, please." He said after several long, silent minutes. Stanley bent forward and undid the bonds on his wrists without hesitating. Terry rubbed at the sore skin. It had healed into a series of fresh pink lines, smooth and fresh. He pulled the IV from his arm and pushed himself up to sitting. It took more work than he'd realized and as the Danish dropped down into his lap, his stomach made a loud grumble.

"Easy, Terry. It took time for you to recover. You used up more energy than you should have. You're not getting enough sleep so you're not letting yourself recover naturally. If you keep pushing yourself like this, you're going to use too much of yourself and burn away."

"I've seen burn out, Stanley. You don't have to lecture me. I'm not a child anymore." He took a large bite of the Danish and let himself give a small moan of delight. It was, at that moment, the best tasting piece of soggy cardboard he'd ever eaten.

"You haven't seen it like this," Stanley chided. His voice took on the cold tone of a lecture, hard and precise. "You've seen exhausted burn out. You've seen Blue Eye's explosive burn out. You've never seen what happens when a key bearer blasts past the point of no return. You aren't in the rookie leagues anymore. You have two of them, Terry. If you lose control, if you use either key too much, you're going to tear the veil. And it isn't going to be a small rip that can be mended by dancing sheets!"

Stanley stood up and leaned down to look at Terry face-to-face. He had always been a foot taller than his student, and the weary lines at the corners of his steely eyes added to size. He pushed his face close enough that their noses almost touched and through clenched teeth said, "Do you understand what I'm saying? You are not a Galahad. You are not invincible, and your stubborn refusal to accept that is a threat to the veil. How many Midnight Mages are left? How many of them do you think you can fight? Are you as arrogant as the old men you claim to hate?"

"Okay! I get it!" Terry tried to meet the hard stare with defiant eyes, but he balked and dropped his gaze to the ground. He felt his posture slump forward. "I try," he said quietly. "But there isn't anyone else, Stanley. When was the last time someone had to carry two keys? When was the last time a key bearer was completely alone without Order support? It's not like it was before the war. There's me, and then behind me, there's seven billion people. I'm the only thing standing between them and the titans. I'm the only one. Those other mages you're talking about? Where the fuck are they? Huh? What are they doing? I'm alone."

"You have an apprentice," Stanley said, standing back up straight.

"Who is sixteen and thinks he's ready to take on the entire world."

"When you were sixteen, you'd already fought in the war."

"Christ!" Terry took a deep breath. "He's got two years of training. By the time the war started, I'd been in active combat training longer than that. He's not ready for these kinds of fights yet, if he ever will be."

"What about Slate? Or the avatar? The artificer? You have allies."

111

"Slate was there. He was about as useful as I was. The only thing that saved us was the fucking construct. We got lucky with Neil. I got lucky. Once. And I've just been feeding Slate's team whatever knowledge they ask for ever since. I'm a glorified Google, and really, Munindwade does all of that work, anyway. I don't know what I'm doing."

"Want some advice from someone that's been there?" Stanley sat back down, suddenly seeming very small and frail again.

"Yes!" Terry blurted. "Of course! Tell me what to do!"

"I can't tell you what to do," Stanley said. "But I can tell you what I'd do." He waited, letting the air grow tense with anticipation the same way he had when he was still teaching classes. When Terry and Munindwade both began to lean forward, he finally continued. "I'd gather my allies." He stood up and moved to the door. "I'd find the person that murdered my friend. Then, I'd decide the most important decision you will ever make. Are you a Guardian, or are you a Sentinel. There is a difference."

He closed the door behind him with a soft click and was gone. Terry stared after him for several moments before finally turning to look down at Munindwade resting at the foot of the bed, licking at the glazed frosting at the sides of his mouth.

"Did any of that make sense to you at all?" Terry asked. Munindwade shook his head. "What the fuck is the difference between a guardian and a sentinel?"

Munindwade shrugged, pulled the last cupcake from the bag, then triumphantly announced, "I know! Spelling!"

CHAPTER 20

It was several interminable hours later when Terry was finally allowed another visitor. The doctors came and went several times, getting increasingly agitated at his refusal to allow them to put the IV back in his arm. Terry spent the time between their visits focusing on the meditation techniques that David had taught him, reaching down into the Earth and pulling the life deep within it back up into himself without causing immediate harm to the plants in the area. It was a slow, laborious process, and Munindwade kept interrupting him, but by the time Slate and Gabriel finally showed up to take him home, he had almost completely recovered from the burns that had made their way up his arm and shoulder.

He was more eager for the duffle bag full of clothes they brought him than he was for their company. He changed out of the open-backed hospital gown into a clean pair of slacks and a long-sleeved t-shirt with glee, happy to once again feel human.

"I wonder if we could figure out a way to bottle that ability," Slate said as Terry pulled the shirt on over his head. "I bet every housewife in the US would pay a month's rent to have instant smooth skin like that."

"Half the house-husbands, too," Gabriel supplied. "Not sure it's worth the setup, though. Did David teach you that?"

"Yeah," Terry said. He sat down on the bed to pull on his socks and shoes. "It's a good one, you should both learn it." He broke one of the fraying shoestrings on his old, worn out Converse sneakers and sighed. "I'm going to have to get some new shoes, aren't I?" He poked at the hole near his big toe. "Seems like everything I have is getting worn out." He tied off the broken lace in a double knot and pushed himself to his feet. "Let's get out of here."

"Terry, we need to talk," Slate said, moving to block the door. "You should know what's happened while you were out."

"It's been a few hours, Jared. How much could have happened?"

Slate and Gabriel exchanged a look, and Slate took a deep breath. "You've been down for three days. Didn't any of the doctors say anything?"

"Mostly they just backed away slowly when I threatened to let Munindwade eat their testicles if they kept trying to inject me with poison," Terry said. "Seriously though, three days?"

Slate nodded. "And a lot has happened. After Roderick's monster survived the fire, and carried you out barely alive to boot, it got some attention."

"Okay. So, what? It won a medal or something? It doesn't matter, Slate. I'm going to break it. And then I'm going to break the pieces. And then I'll probably smash those broken pieces into powder."

"It's not that simple," Slate said. "The Pentagon has decided not to let an asset like Max slip through their fingers. He's going to start mass producing those things for the US Military soon."

"You've got to be fucking with me, right?" Terry's hand tightened of its own volition. "He's committed at least three murders. He's going down, Slate. I won't let him just walk away with a shiny new prize and give the US Government the ability to build those abominations."

"No," Slate said with a tight voice. "He's technically exorcised four spirits, which, might I add, is my team's job. You included."

Terry swallowed back his retort, took a deep breath and huffed it out through his nose. "Fine." He started toward the door. "Come on, Gabriel. The United States Government clearly wants to up its nuclear arsenal at the expense of the American people. We'll just have to try Roderick for his violations of the OSS's laws." He stopped next to Slate. "He'll get a fair trial, I'm sure."

"Wait, Terry." Slate put his hand against Terry's chest and pushed him back into the room. "If you try and go after him, I'll be forced to bring you in. You'll lose your contract. You probably will go to prison. You might get executed. How will that help anyone?"

"You do what you have to do, Jared. I have a job, one I do without getting paid, and that job is keeping you all alive. Max's actions have seriously jeopardized that. You think a massive Salamander like like that could just bust through to our side all on his own? No. He can only be summoned. That means Max opened a gate somehow, probably using magi-tech he stole from Leigh, though God alone knows why she'd have built something like that in the first place. If you think for a second I'm going to let some entitled trust-fund fucktard get away with tugging at the edges of the veil on my watch, you're as stupid as he is."

"You owe me twenty bucks," Gabriel said, holding a hand out to Slate.

Slate reached into his pocket and pulled out a twenty dollar bill from his wallet. He handed it to Gabriel, muttering under his breath, "Gambling is a sin, you know."

"You'd be surprised what we're allowed to do with money when it comes to you gentiles." Gabriel pocketed the twenty and smiled. "Now, I can get a Frappuccino and Sue won't ever have to know."

"I'm pretty sure you're not supposed to lie to your fiancé, either."

"What the fuck are you guys talking about?" Terry asked. He crossed his arms over his chest and looked back and forth between the two of them. "Did I miss something? Did I suffer brain damage?"

"I bet Jared $20 that you would go off half-cocked and risk ruining the plan before you ever even found out about it." Gabriel explained. "He even brought in Stanley to try and hedge his bet, but in the end, I knew I could rely on you to be an irrational, angry jerk."

"So, we are going to arrest Max?" Terry asked.

"No, he really is untouchable like that," Slate said. "But, we can make sure he wished he was dead. Come on. Everyone's waiting for us. Let's get out of this death factory before we all come down with airborne herpes or something."

Terry picked Munindwade up from the floor and sat him on his shoulder. He eyed the homunculus suspiciously. "You were in on this, weren't you?"

Munindwade nodded. "I really thought you'd just start cutting holes in the wall hours ago. Want the key back?"

Terry nodded, and Munindwade opened his mouth, reached down his throat with one hand and pulled the black key up from inside him by the chain. Terry grimaced as he wiped little pieces of donut from it, and then slipped it back over his neck with a shiver. "From now on, you don't get food."

Munindwade made a whining groan as they walked out of the hospital room and on to freedom.

CHAPTER 21

They pulled up to the ranch house a half hour later. Terry was relieved to see that his own car was parked next to David's in the driveway, pinned in behind Leigh's compact SUV. Slate parked in the street and they all climbed out into the cool evening. Terry shivered slightly in the wet, cold breeze and wondered why no one had thought to at least bring him a jacket.

"You got my keys?" he asked.

Gabriel pulled them from his pants pocket and tossed them over to him. "You're not planning on taking off on us are you?"

"Nah, I just want to grab some things from my trunk. I'll be inside in just a second. Terry pushed the button on his key fob, and the truck thunked open. He waited for the other two to head inside, and then pulled the latch open. He moved some things around inside and lifted the piece of thin wood that covered the compartment where his spare tire was supposed to be. Underneath, the lining of his trunk was filled with small tools he'd moved from Stanley's trunk. The iron gargoyle that had served as the treasure's guardian had been relocated to a new duty, making sure no one was able to get into the small safe sitting atop his refrigerator at home.

"Take the big one," Munindwade said, hopping down into the trunk from his shoulder. "You never use the big one!"

Terry snickered and pulled his backpack from the trunk. "I don't think I need anything like that, but I am definitely tired of getting my ass kicked by that thing. I want some padding." He slung the backpack over his shoulder and put the board back in place. "Come on, let's go inside before they think we've taken off on a mission of vengeance."

Munindwade made a clicking noise with his tongue as Terry lifted him out of the trunk and closed it. "Just once, I'd like to see us smash something with overwhelming force."

Terry shrugged. "I think everything we do is overkill. I'm tired of hunting squirrels with an assault rifle."

"But, Terry," Munindwade whined. "Tiny isn't a squirrel, he's a rhinoceros."

"We'll see." Terry walked up the flat stone path to the front door and before going inside turned to face Munindwade. "Muni, I might have an errand for you."

"You want the really big one, don't you?"

Terry nodded. "Yeah, I don't think I'll need it, but, Boy Scout's motto and all that." He pushed the door open and stepped inside to find his friends sitting in the living room gathered around the coffee table. Leigh was explaining the four stone jars sitting in the middle, and Terry took a step back into the hall. The jars buzzed with a desperate need and Terry had to struggle to not rush over to them. "Is that what I think it is?"

"Yes," Leigh said. She rubbed at her elbow and didn't meet his eyes as she spoke. "It's the last of the original batch."

Terry shook his head and took another step back. "Get rid of it."

"I can't, Terry. I need it to fuel the plan."

"I don't care. I can't be around it." His hands itched and he forced himself to take another step down the hall. "I... need a cigarette." He stormed out through the kitchen, pulling the pack from his pocket and lighting the first one before he'd even closed the door behind him. He looked up to find Trish sitting on the edge of the patio in one of the camp chairs and quickly moved out into the yard. Terry mumbled a short, "Sorry" as he walked past her, doing his best to keep the smoke away from the pregnant woman.

Terry leaned against the fence and took several long drags. He didn't like being that close to the drug again. Just knowing that it was sitting on the table in the other room brought all kinds of uncomfortable thoughts running to the surface. He finished the first cigarette and lit a second one from the smoldering butt before snuffing it beneath his heel. When he looked up, he noticed that Trish had turned her chair around to watch him.

"What?" he barked.

"You've done it," she said as if it were the most obvious ting in the world.

"Done what?" he asked. He took another heavy drag and let the smoke just roll out of his mouth like a waterfall.

"Blue Eye," she said. "You've done it. I know. I can always recognize the look of a fellow addict." She pushed herself up from the chair, leading with her belly in the way pregnant women always seem to do. She walked to the edge of the patio and leaned against the support beam. "Want to talk about it?"

"I didn't even realize you were a practitioner," Terry said. He put the second cigarette out without finishing it and walked over to stand beside her. "And no, I don't."

She shrugged. "I'm not anymore. But once, I was a recruit in Unending Sea, and I thought I needed an edge to make it through the induction ritual."

"Yeah?" Terry's eyes perked up and he examined her in a new light. "You wanted to be a crystal-gazer?"

"Better than a vampire, right?" She chuckled. "I just wanted to study spirits. I always have. I would probably have made it, too, if it wasn't for the war. They got a lot pickier about who was let in after Muborak. I had to get a lot stronger if I was going to make the cut, so, Blue Eye."

"You know, you don't have to be in an Order to study spirits anymore. You can get a lot of information from Google, and there are some colleges out east that are starting Meta-zoology departments. Hell, some of them probably even have some wet dogs teaching them."

She waved at her stomach. "Might be a little hard these days, but you never know. Mostly, though, I'm just a spiritual witch. I don't miss magic all that much."

121

"That's cool," Terry said. He fumbled for a way to keep the friendly conversation going. It was the longest he'd ever managed to talk to her without offending her in some way, and he wanted it to last as long as it could before he inevitably screwed it up. "So, are you like, an old school pagan, or a new-wave Wiccan?"

"I guess I'd be a neo-pagan? But I don't really define it. It's hard to see the traditions without the context. I just kind of take what I like from where I like it and go with that."

"So, big important question, then, Odin or Pan?"

"Odin! Dude's basically Santa Claus with a spear. What's not to worship?"

They shared a laugh and Terry shook his head to bring some of his mind back to the forefront. "I'm sorry," he said quietly, looking away from her.

"Because Odin's a bad-ass? No need to apologize for that. It's completely true."

Terry smiled. "No, I'm sorry I've been such a dick to you."

"Oh." She looked him over appraisingly. "Well, you can't help it. You're an asshole. I'm a bitch. The world probably couldn't handle us if we were too friendly."

"You have any idea what they've got planned?" He asked hesitantly. He wasn't sure how much David had brought her into the fold, or how much he wanted her to be a part of it.

"No, you?"

He shook his head. "Whatever it is, if taking Blue Eye is part of the plan, it's a bad one."

A strange look slid across her face, one Terry didn't recognize. He realized as he expression changed that he couldn't sense what she was feeling in any way. He'd grown used to the background hum of emotions in the past couple of years, and now he finally realized why he was so uncomfortable around her for so long. She must have caught some glimpse of his thoughts on his face because she just grinned at him and said, "Burn out."

"What?"

"I'm a burn out. There's not even enough juice left for an aura. That's why you can't read me."

"Can you read minds?" Terry asked. It was possible. If she'd been in the Unending Sea, she could have easily learned it. Knowledge, especially in its most secret forms, was what they did.

She shook her head. "No, but David is my baby daddy. I know the look an Empath gets when they realize for the first time why someone makes their skin crawl."

"You're not like, dead inside, or anything, are you?" Terry blurted out.

She chuckled again. "Blunt. Nice. No, I'm not dead inside. I just don't have that field that makes it easy to connect to other people. It's like I'm wearing that stuff hunters use to mask their scent from deer. You have to get pretty close to ever notice my smell."

"Impregnation close?"

"Well, good time close at least," she admitted.

He caught her eyes and she grinned at him and raised her eyebrows. "You're diiiiiiirty," he said, drawing out the last word in a sing-song voice.

"I do not apologize for liking sex."

"Power to you."

"Power to me."

The glass door slid open and Suez stepped out of the house onto the patio. He smiled a toothy smile at Trish, the stood before Terry with his hands folded in a pale imitation of begging. Terry rolled his eyes and handed him the pack of cigarettes. Suez bounced on the balls of his feet, pulled one out and announced, "You, sir, are a god among men."

Trish looked between the two of them and moved to the door. "I think I'll go check on David," she gave Terry a smile as she stepped inside and closed the door behind her.

Terry lit Suez's cigarette and pulled out his own. "I can't be around it, Sue. You know that."

"This is the plan, Terry. We're going to do this, with or without you. I'd rather you be there, but if you don't want to be a part of it, fine. But this is about more than just one spirit. Have you thought about what will happen if these things go into global production? Drones will look like a joke by comparison. My people will be in danger. I won't let that happen."

"Why not? America, fuck yeah."

Suez took a drag off the cigarette, "You don't get it. Why do you think Roderick built the construct in the first place? He designed the entire thing with one target in mind. Then, that target graciously and voluntarily field tested it, over and over again. You helped him work out the bugs."

Terry laughed. "You think the US government commissioned a magic death robot to kill me? That's just, well, stupid. If some general wanted me dead, he could get Slate to do it easy. I wouldn't even see it coming."

"You're being too short sighted." Suez tilted his head to one side, looking off into space at something Terry couldn't see. "Right now, there's just under one thousand potential targets. Not counting, of course, the potential, potential targets, like the people they train or the new talent that's coming up in the world. Within a few years, unchecked, that number will grow to over a million. Look how much we've grown right here in the Ozarks. You think someone is just going to let that go? No. Roderick is only the first person to come up with a workable solution and he sure won't be the last. We have to make a point now."

Terry watched the hard, sharp lines of his face as he spoke. There was no emotion to his words, no passion. It was just simple fact. He was watching the possibilities play out. "You're not fucking with me, are you?"

Suez shook his head. "No." He finished the cigarette and tossed the butt out into the yard. "Things are going to get worse before they get better. People are desperate. It's a whole new world."

"Do the others know?" Terry asked.

"Slate's an insider. He's got to have figured it out on his own. Gabriel could, but won't let himself see that dark side of humanity. I think Leigh knows. I think she saw it coming before the war even ended." Suez slid the door open. "Come on. Leigh's plan is pretty good. It might even work."

Terry tossed the remainder of his cigarette out into the yard and followed Suez inside. "Is it wrong that I feel weird about her being smarter than me?" he asked, only half-joking.

"If you're bothered by people being smarter than you," Suez said with a smile, "I'm surprised you can bear to be around anyone at all."

CHAPTER 22

A half-hour later, Terry found himself standing in the door to Gabriel and Suez's garage watching as Leigh put the finishing touches on her special project. He was amazed by how much work she'd managed to cram into a handful of days. The construct stood in the middle of the concrete floor, its slick black skin shinning in the florescent work lights. The sharp angles of its bulkier armor plating at the chest, shoulders and joints flowed smoothly over the soft curves of its under body. As he watched, Leigh finished etching something into its shoulder and waved him over.

"I still can't believe you built a fucking Knight Saber," he said as he walked in a wide arch around the room, careful to avoid coming too near the stone jars sitting off to one side. "Did you go with knuckle-bombers or head-whips?"

"Neither," Leigh said. She picked up the first stone bottle. "I didn't have time to give her anything but raw, brute strength and a big ole dollop of speed. If Munindwade is right about what Tiny is capable of, she should come through alright."

"He is." Terry bent down to inspect the symbol she had carved in the construct's upper arm. There were three images, the first was a stylized butterfly L that he had come to recognize as her personal branding, the second was the lined hills that he'd seen on several of the Ozark Spiritual Sovereignty's most recent documents, and finally, underlying both of those was the outline of a tower and crescent moon. It was the same symbol she'd embroidered on his coat when she'd made it for him years before. It wasn't the official symbol of the Order of Midnight, but it had that meaning all the same. "You're throwing down the gauntlet on this, aren't you?"

"We have to stand up, right, make our names known. If we don't, they're just going to come back at us again. Did Sue tell you that some people in Utah are trying to declare independence, too? It's only a matter of time until the US decides we no longer have that right. It's now-or-never, do-or-die time."

"It's the dying part I'm not too excited about," Terry muttered. "You don't have to take it, you know. Suez and I could charge her up to capacity, I think."

"No offense, Terry, but no, you couldn't." Leigh pulled the cork from the bottle. The sweet smell of over-ripe fruit wafted up. The heady perfume made Terry's skin crawl with anticipation. It was different from the smell he remembered, stronger and sweeter, more like rotting cantaloupe than rotting bananas. "Blue Eye is liquid potential. It's dangerous, but it can be controlled if you know what you're doing." She raised the jar to her lips and tipped it back. She let the azure liquid slide down her throat in one

128

long chug then sat the empty jar down and picked up the second. A gasp escaped her lips as she stood back up and her cheeks burned rosy. A buzz of energy started to float off of her skin, little sparks flickering off the hair on her arms.

She closed her eyes and took a deep breath before downing the second bottle. When she opened her eyes again, the signature cyan glow radiated out of her irises, visible even in the bright florescent shop lights. Mist of the same cyan color began to dance off her skin, giving her face the distorted look of being on the other side of a fish tank.

"Alright," she said. Her voice warbled with a slight anamorphic reverberation that echoed in her mouth. "One more and we'll be ready to do this." She popped the cork on the last jar and downed it without ceremony. Showers of static poured from her hair as it stood up on her head. Strands clicked and snapped as they bounced into one another. The blue mist rolled off of her face and hands and the bright light shining in her eyes became painful to look at.

Terry could feel the heat coming off of her. He knew first hand that the mist was her irradiated sweat evaporating as quickly as it could escape her pores. The torrent of screaming, primal emotions in the back of his mind tore at him and he had to force himself to not grab her and pull the drug out of her. His hands shook as he watched her work, need and jealousy weighing heavily on him.

She ran one hand across the heavy chest plate and the construct shuddered to life. Light seeped through cracks he hadn't known were there as the front of the construct began to split away from the back, revealing the hollow interior, custom designed to hold Leigh's frame. Leigh stepped between the two halves, pushing her feet down into the boots and thrusting each hand into the gloves. "She's powered directly off my excess burn," she echoed. "She'll draw off the power the same way you do, sucking it out and using it to fuel her systems."

The construct hissed as it slid closed around her. Leigh's face became visible behind the transparent mask of its featureless face. The edges of the plates began to pulse with the blue glow of the power the construct drew from its pilot, and a moment later, all of it faded back to solid, smooth black and Leigh's face disappeared behind the mask again.

"I am Iron Man," Leigh said, her voice twisted by the construct into a rumbling baritone. "I kick ass and take names."

"If you're going to indulge in the referential one-liners, you have to keep them to one line," Terry said with a laugh.

"Maybe you do," Leigh boomed. "But that limitation only exists on the Y-chromosome."

CHAPTER 23

The sun had already dropped behind the horizon by the time they pulled into the parking lot of the Meta-Crimes offices. The black skin of Leigh's construct seemed to draw in the orange glow of the street lights, darkening its entire form into one smooth shadow. Terry walked next to her, his own armor jingling as he moved. He was aware of the strange juxtaposition of her sleek, cyberpunk aesthetic and his more traditional appearance. He tightened the fingerless leather gauntlets and wondered if it was time to add some spiked studs or something to the chain mail and leather.

"Armor envy?" David asked from behind him. "Now, I've seen it all."

"I'm not jealous," Terry lied. "I've got a classic look. Cultivated for generations."

"If Christopher Lambert's Beowulf is a classic, I don't want to live in this world anymore." David smiled a toothy smile and lifted the ten pound bag of black sand. "How big do you want it?"

"I can do a good hundred feet. More than that, and I don't know what will be able to come through." David nodded and jogged off to the side of the parking lot to begin pouring the sand in a wide arc on the asphalt. "Are you sure he's going to be here?" Terry asked, turning to Slate.

"Yes. They're scheduled to pick him up here in about fifteen minutes. According to Chad he's been here since about fifteen-hundred-hours gathering personal belongings from the rubble of the lab."

"So we wait for the army guys to show up, Leigh puts the smack down on Tiny and then we all go for chicken fingers. Easy-peasy-lemon-squeezy."

Terry walked away from the group and leaned against the hood of his car to watch David's circle being constructed. He did the math in his head and let out a huff of breath.

"Will five minutes be enough?" Munindwade asked through the passenger window. He was leaning out of the car, doing the same calculations with concerned eyes. "It might take longer than that."

"It'll be enough. Any longer than five minutes of exertion and Leigh risks full burn-out anyway. We don't want to be around if that happens." Terry lit a cigarette and took a drag. "I should be the one doing this."

"Yes." Munindwade said without hesitation.

"Thanks buddy. That makes me feel infinitely better."

"Let's go over Tiny's weaknesses one more time," Slate called. "We know most of the tricks Terry's used on it before won't be very effective. Roderick has done a lot of work with the data and has managed to counter each tactic with the newest iteration for months now."

"Well, that means you're not going to be able to drain the power or chop it up with Soulbinder." The scene at the loft broke into Terry's mind and he added, "Or blasting it apart. I'd imagine it can take a pretty good licking and keep on ticking, too. If Saddy couldn't break it, it's probably not going to have a hard time shrugging off some pretty good hits."

"So, what does that leave us with?" Slate asked.

"The controls," Leigh said. "The circle is going to cut off Roderick's remote. He'll either have to get into the fight to control it close range or see if it can fight on its own."

"I don't know," Terry said. "It didn't seem to have any problem with the salamanders and unless Roddy has a fire-proof surveillance system in the gym that we don't know about, he couldn't have been feeding it commands."

"That's good," Leigh assured him. "If it's got automation, it's got personality. That means it has at least something like a mind of its own. Have you ever heard the myth of the golem? They do not like being controlled. They make great guardians, but they can be hell if they get loose."

"Says the woman currently wearing one," Slate added.

"We've got one other advantage," Leigh continued, ignoring him. "His batteries keep breaking. He's overtaxing the stones. That means he's on a time limit in the fight. I'm going to do my best to target the power source, force him to protect that. I'm guessing the stones are in its head or chest. Just from a design standpoint it makes sense."

133

"So we follow the plan," Terry said. "Controls and power."

"And protecting innocent bystanders," Slate added. "I've seen the transformer movies. I know the type of collateral damage that happens when robots fight."

"Yeah, but those guys are, what, five stories or something? No worries here." Terry assured him.

Slate gave him a flat stare. "I've watched Japanimation, too, you know."

"No one calls it that anymore. It's anime now."

Slate's reply got cut off as the rumble of a large truck engine roared onto the street. The olive drab deuce-and-a half came thumping into the parking lot a moment later, hissing to a stop beside Terry's car. The passenger door opened and an older man with a buzz cut wearing an ACU jumped down from the cab.

Slate waved in greeting and started to walk over to him, but the colonel waved him off. "Not again, Agent. It's been decided. We're not going to hear any more arguments about crimes against non-humans. We protect the citizens of the United States, and until Congress decides otherwise, that only includes the flesh-and-blood men and women."

"Well, we've got a problem with that," Terry said. He jogged over the man and bent forward in a show of examining the little eagle on his shoulder. "Sargent."

Slate rolled his eyes and pushed Terry back behind him. "Colonel," he pointedly corrected, "we understand the importance of this project for

Homeland Security and the DOD, but, before we give a man like Roderick significant resources, we thought we should at least explore the accusation that he's a fraud."

"Why is this the first time I'm hearing about this?" The colonel asked. "Who's making these accusations?"

"The original designer of the construct, its power supply and the rest of the magi-tech it's based on," Terry said. "She asserts that Roderick bought a storage locker containing her failed experiments and flawed inventions and is trying to pawn them off on the US Government." Terry gestured to Leigh and she walked smoothly across the parking lot in a fluid, graceful march. "She claims the advanced model can wipe the floor a thousand times over with Roderick's knock-off prototype design."

Leigh stopped beside him, clicked her heels together and saluted the colonel with one raised hand. "A little much?" Terry whispered, and Leigh dropped her hand to her side.

"Is this a joke?" The colonel asked. He turned back to Slate. "You expect me to suspend operations while you investigate this claim?"

Slate shook his head. "Of course not. If what Howard says is true, then we can find out tonight."

"How do you propose we do that?"

Terry stepped up again, raising one finger as he announced, "Robot Thunderdome! Two bots enter, one bot leaves! We want you to let our robot fight Roderick's robot to the disassemble. If your guy wins, it's one more feather in Roderick's hat. If our guy wins, the creator is willing to negotiate one of those lucrative government contracts we're always hearing about on MS-NBC."

"Colonel, we have a time table," the soldier in the driver's seat said. Terry held his breath. He could sense the curiosity in the colonel's mind working its way up. It started to slide back down, but a wave slid over them from across the parking lot as David pulled at the colonel's natural instincts and forced him into decisiveness.

"Alright," he said. "I want to see this play out. Why not? We'll let the robots duke it out, but I don't want any interference here." He glared at Terry pointedly. "No offense, son, but you've got a bit of a reputation for shenanigans."

Terry ran his fingers over his chest. "Cross-my-heart-hope-to-die," he said. "I wouldn't do anything to violate the accords between my Order and the United States Government."

"Simmons," the colonel barked to the soldier waiting in the truck. "Go fetch Dr. Roderick. We've got a tight schedule. It's a long drive back to Fort Leonard Wood."

Simmons hopped down from the truck, saluted, and headed off inside in a hurry. A few minutes passed, and he reemerged from the burned building, leading Roderick and the construct. He carried the tile-board controls under one arm and held the strap of a duffle-bag on his shoulder with the other.

"This is a joke, right Terry? You can't possibly have built something that challenges Tiny in a few days. It takes years of work to build something like this. You don't just put it together in a garage overnight."

Terry shrugged and gestured to Leigh. She walked out to the middle of the circle laid out on the parking lot and bowed to the construct.

Max sighed and tossed his duffle-bag into the back of the truck. "If I have to do this, let's make it quick." He flipped the tiles on the board and fell in beside the colonel. The construct's eyes lit up and it raised its arms to pounce. Leigh lowered herself down into a defensive position and nodded.

"Alright," Max said. "Let's rock and roll." He pushed a tile forward on the board and the construct charged.

CHAPTER 24

Tiny threw its arms wide as it ran forward. Leigh let it barrel into her, waiting until the arms started to close around her chest before dropping smoothly into a roll. She popped up behind the construct, spinning on the toes of one foot in a graceful pirouette. She stood in that pose, arms raised, right foot pressed against her left knee and waited.

"What kind of fighting style is that thing programmed with?" The colonel asked.

"I'm pretty sure that would be Eastern European Ballet," Terry sniped. "No deadlier art has ever been imagined by the likes of man."

The colonel looked at him with skeptical eyes but Terry just stared back at him blankly. "If you're not going to take this seriously, you're either right about Dr. Roderick's work or you're even more insane than your file suggests."

Terry shrugged. "We'll see, won't we?"

The colonel turned back to watch the fight with a derisive sneer on his face. Terry ignored him, instead watching Leigh dance around the slow, heavy construct. She moved with quick, graceful arcs, stopping between each motion to pose. Terry realized she needed those few seconds to reorient herself after each burst of speed. She would let the armor guide her movements for a few short bursts and then take control again when the immediate danger had passed. She was doing her best to keep the burn of the Blue Eye to a minimum. He'd have to see if he could help her with that.

He knelt down next to the ring of sand and fiddled with the strings on his shoe. Without looking down, he reached out with his right hand and touched the sand with the tips of his fingers. A spark of energy flowed out of him into the barrier as it snapped into place with an invisible, intangible wall.

Tiny stopped moving immediately, freezing in place as the commands from the tile board were cut off. Leigh took advantage. She leaped onto the construct's back and dug her fingers into the stony shoulders. The seams on her armor began to glow as she jerked on the armor along the constructs back. Her strained voice came out in a heavy grunt as the fake-stone pulled away exposing the poly-carbonate armor beneath.

"You cheated!" Max shouted.

"I warned you," the colonel said, rounding on Terry. "No shenanigans!"

Terry rolled his eyes. "You know how many fights that thing is going to get into without being confined in some sort of circle? None. Standard practice when mages fight, build a barrier to prevent collateral damage. Our robot is still functioning. If his can't handle that, then he should go fuck himself."

"Wait!" Roderick pleaded. "I can get it running again. I've got a plan for this sort of thing." He ran over to where Leigh was standing still, examining the inner workings of the construct. He shoulder his way past her and opened the inner chest by sliding something on the tile board. He pulled a few of the tiles free from the board and slid them into sockets beside the four spirit stones.

"There," he said as he pushed the chest closed again. "Now, we'll see if your little toy ballerina can handle a fight without you cheating."

"Time for round two," Terry muttered. He took a step over the line of sand and focused on the energy inside the circle. The barrier changed from invisible to a dome made of red heat-shimmers. Oil started to seep up through the asphalt as the air grew steadily warmer. Terry walked out into the middle of the circle, spinning the black key around his hand by the chain. "Okay Roddy, how about we make this interesting?"

Roderick's eyes widened as the dome began to turn solid red and heat began to radiate off of it in waves. "What did you do?" he demanded in a squeaky, panicked voice.

"Here's the deal," Terry said. He pulled a cigarette from his pocket and lit it. "You've got two options at this point. You can admit that you're a murderer and a fraud." He took a drag from the cigarette for a dramatic pause and then blew the smoke out through his nose. It slowly sunk to the ground at his feet. "Or, you can rely on your tinker toy to protect you."

"You threatening me, Terry?" Roderick squeaked. "The colonel ordered you not to interfere."

140

Terry shrugged. "Funny thing, I don't actually take orders from him." He dropped the cigarette into the pool of smoke below him. It bounced from the surface as if striking solid ground, embers from the cherry spreading out in little piles of fire. "But, I'm not interfering, right? I'm Switzerland. Completely neutral." The sparks and smoke began to swirl, spreading out in a thin line across the entire circle. "Papa Inferno, though. That's the Salamander King, by the way. He might be a little biased."

The asphalt began to smoke on its own as the oil bubbled up from the tar and burned off. It rose to the top of the dome in thick, acrid plumes and began to gather back down, forming the shape of a large frog tall enough to barely fit inside the dome.

"Do you know where you fucked up, Roddy?" Terry asked.

"I should have used a shell company when I bought the hippy's storage locker?"

"No, you stupid piece of shit." Terry backed away from the gathering smoke, retreating to the far side of the circle. "You thought stealing power made you powerful. Take it from a professional tick, you fuck with fire and you get burned."

The smoke hardened and turned crimson, forming completely into the body of the Lord of the Pyrophibians. Papa Inferno stood close to forty-foot-tall and was wider again by half. His flame coated hide rippled in the air as he let out a powerful croaking roar. "You summoned me, little vampire? Are you ready for justice to be served?"

"Yes, actually." Terry answered. He pointed at Roderick cringing behind the construct. "That goat fucker over there is responsible for Saddy's death. His golem is also what slaughtered your children a few days ago. I'm sure you can smell the power seeping out of it. He's not under my protection. I can't interfere."

The massive elemental leaned down and sniffed at the construct. "You're right. I smell mud and weeds. Fish and bugs. I smell blood and water."

"Go, Go!" Roderick shouted, shrinking back. The construct's eyes lit up again and it took a defensive stance between him and the Salamander King.

"You think your toy is going to stand a chance against me?" The elemental stepped forward and chuffed a clicking laugh. "You aren't catching me off guard, artificer. I'm not a youth. I'm not a tired old lady. I am a warrior."

He raised one massive webbed hand and smashed it down on the construct, pinning it to the ground. The elemental leaned its face forward to stare at Roderick, blinked its eyes then flicked out its tongue.

A heartbeat later, a screaming Roderick disappeared into the massive mouth.

CHAPTER 25

The giant elemental laughed as Roderick's screams continued to bubble up from its mouth. The creature was keeping him alive for the pure pleasure of it. Terry's stomach tightened, but he couldn't force himself to look away. "Alright," he said quietly. "You got what you wanted. Now leave."

The bullfrog turned to him, ignoring the construct lying on the ground. It lowered its massive face to ground level, bringing its eyes down to narrow on Terry. "Are you commanding me, tick? You don't have a deal with me. You brought me here and I'm going to stay."

"No, you're not." Terry spun the chain around his hand again, wrapping it until the key slapped into his palm. He raised his hand, feeling the weight of the sword as it formed. "Last chance. This is my circle. I make the rules here."

An explosion of laughter echoed up from the massive elemental. It flung out one quick flick of its paw and smashed the surrounding dome. Sand lurched into the air, instantly liquefying into chunks of molten glass. "What circle?" It rose up to its full height, no longer encumbered by the confines of the dome. It croaked out a roar of challenge and flames sparked up along its skin.

Fear choked off Terry's next sentence as the bullfrog bulged out its chest. He took a step forward, raising the sword and steadying himself for what came next. The frog made a sickening hocking noise and spit the ball of liquid fire. Terry closed his eyes against the heat and braced himself.

Something hard hit him from behind. He felt himself tossed through the air, crashing down on the asphalt a few yards away. He looked up in time to see the ball of magma splatter over Leigh's armor in smoking, sizzling globs. She stood through it as if she'd be hit with a water balloon, completely unfazed. She swept a thick red slime off her shoulder then tilted her head to one side, starring up at Papa Inferno.

"Hey, slime dick," she boomed through the armor. "You're going to have to do better than that."

"It thinks," the salamander king slithered, "It has a mind. Very dangerous, tick... very troubling."

Leigh reached up and touched the side of the helmet, turning the face-plate transparent again. "You've got bigger problems than that, big guy." She dropped into a low crouch, fists raised. "I'm going to rip you apart."

"Objective Redirect." Roderick's construct rumbled from the asphalt. "Clean Sweep Protocol Activated. Assessing Threat."

Terry ignored it, watching as Leigh charged into the giant elemental. The seams on her armor were glowing again, and he knew she was burning a lot of energy now to keep it going. She moved with an awe inspiring speed, ripping her fists into the salamander's flesh and leaving behind

144

dozens of oozing wounds. The thick slimy blood burst into flames as it hit the asphalt oil and black smoke began to roll up around them.

It was a losing fight, and Terry knew it. The hit and run tactic would work on most living things, but Elementals were not exactly living creatures. You couldn't bleed one out the way you could a person. Terry pushed himself to his feet and shook his muscles loose. He could still hear Roderick's screams echoing inside the elemental. He would have to be careful to not end up in the same position.

Papa Inferno suddenly lunged forward, one massive paw wrapping around Leigh's torso as she darted in on it again. The lights in her armor's seams were fading out and she'd moved to slowly. The frog lifted her off the ground and held her triumphantly in the air. "Another artificer for the fires," it croaked out in a loud, rumbling chuckle.

Terry took the opportunity. He rushed forward, slashing with the sword in an overhead arc with both hands. The blade sunk into the flesh of the salamander's stomach, tearing a long, wide gash across the soft belly. It let out a loud, pained roar and dropped Leigh back to the pavement.

Terry turned and swung the blade again, ignoring the burning pain rising up his arms. The second gouge slid open across the first and the flaps of skin peeled back. Roderick fell from inside the monster, skin blistered and coated in a thick slime. He whimpered and shivered in the cold air, no longer able to scream.

Terry jumped back from the salamander and raised the now glowing sword up into the air. The pain in his hands threatened to crash into him, but he forced himself to ignore his own smoldering flesh and stand his ground. "I warned you, Inferno. You will leave now."

Papa Inferno rocked back on his legs and pushed against the wound in his stomach. The flesh was already beginning to knit itself back together, rivulets of the flaming blood acting as welds across the wounds. It lumbered back from the sight of the sword. Thick smoke began to billow out from its nostrils and mouth as it groaned.

"Threat assessed. Engage primary threat."

Roderick's construct, left mostly ignored on the pavement, suddenly rose to its feet. The hand on the left arm came loose, dropping to the asphalt with a loud thump. It aimed the remaining tube directly at the salamander and braced its body to support the blast. Energy flickered in the air in a soft blue-green swirl that gathered at the tube's tip in a blinding white ball.

The night boomed as the cannon fired. White, purifying light spewed from the construct's arm in a solid, blinding beam that burned the air. It crashed into Papa Inferno tearing through the elemental's muscle and bone, leaving nothing but an afterimage and floating ash.

"Assessing," the construct said as it lowered the cannon and turned back to face the ring.

Terry lowered the sword to his side and examined the skin on his hands. His palms were red and swollen, but hadn't begun to blister yet. He looked over to see David helping Leigh climb out of the now inert armor. She smiled at him with gaunt cheeks and sunken eyes and managed to give

146

a thumbs up before David began dragging her off to the grass. She had used a lot of her own life to keep that fight going, but Terry was sure she would recover.

He wasn't as sure about Roderick. He walked over to the engineer lying in a shivering puddle on the sticky pavement. His skin was covered in burns that left him almost unrecognizable. His hair and clothes were almost entirely burned away. He groaned as Terry leaned down beside him.

"He's still alive!" Terry shouted. "Someone call 911. David! He's alive!"

"Threat assessed. Engage primary threat."

"What?" Terry looked up to see the construct moving toward him. He stood up, backing away from Roderick's prone body. "Hey, there, Tiny. I'm not hurting him big guy."

The construct stopped just on the other side of Roderick's body, raised its left arm, and began to focus energy for the second blast from the cannon.

CHAPTER 26

Terry dove to one side as the pure white light cut the air where his head had been a moment before. He rolled across the asphalt and sprung back to his feet, Soulbinder raised. The construct was tracking his movements, already gathering energy for another blast. After seeing what that cannon had done to the king salamander, Terry was sure he wouldn't like his odds against it.

Sparks flickered off Tiny's head, followed by a series of thunderous barks a half-second later. "Get out of there," Slate shouted. He pulled the trigger again, sending another wave of bullets uselessly cracking into the golem. Tiny turned his cannon to Slate and let the beam fly.

Terry didn't have time to think. He reacted on instinct. He just turned and threw Soulbinder into the path of the beam. The blade collided with the light in an explosion that knocked him from his feet. The sound of metal grinding ripped through the air as the sword began to warp and bend as it drew in the power. It floated in the center of a white vortex for several heartbeats, then the black key clinked to the asphalt, glowing cherry red and smoking at the edge.

The construct hissed as a part of it opened and a broken stone fell to its feet. "Eliminate All Threats." Its head swerved from left to right, pausing as it examined every person in the parking lot. Its gaze settled on Slate and the soldier. The later had produced an assault rifle and was taking careful aim, popping off short bursts of shots that struck the construct's face. Slate, though, had begun loading shells into the large revolver he used in emergencies.

Terry's head swam from the impact with the asphalt. He'd lost concentration and the pain in his hands flared up his arms. He lowered himself back to the ground as the first explosion from Slate's gun rocked the construct back. Terry knew he was out of this fight and probably not getting back in.

"Boy, are you just gonna layabout all day when there's work that needs a doin'?"

Terry opened his eyes and looked up into the face of a young woman bent over to stare him in the face. Her long, white hair hung down around them creating a tunnel from her face to his. "What?" he asked, still dizzy. "I?"

"Get up, boy. That thing's gonna kill your friends and you ain't done fulfilling promises just yet." She brought one long-fingered hand up to her face and stuffed something into her mouth. "A deal's a deal, boy."

"Aunt Saddy?" Terry asked, confused. "What? How?"

"You ain't too bright, are you, boy?" She stood back up and flipped her hair over her shoulder. She towered over him, tall and lean, wrapped in

149

a dress of shimmering crystals tinged with the slightest bit blue. "I swear. Stanley, bless his heart, might just be wrong 'bout you."

Another series of explosions rocked through the night and Roderick's construct tumbled backward onto the pavement. It hissed and popped again, dropping a second fractured stone before pushing itself back to its feet and taking aim with the cannon.

"I have to get back into this fight." Terry pushed himself up to sit at Saddy's feet. "I can't let that thing go on a killing spree."

"It ain't your job to stop it. It ain't a threat to the veil."

Terry shook his head. "Doesn't matter." He forced himself up to his feet and stumbled a bit as his head spun. He took a deep breath and forced his mind to focus through the pain.

"It's gonna be the death of you."

"Probably," He rolled his shoulders and took a slow step forward a little less wobbly this time.

"Yep," Saddy said. "You're a guardian." She reached out with one hand and touched his chest. Ice cold stung at his skin and he jerked the second chain out from under his shirt. The white key hung there, slightly covered in frost. She nodded at him, touched the key and vanished.

"Alright," Terry said as the pain washed out of him. He grabbed the key with his left hand and pulled the chain all the way off. "Round three."

CHAPTER 27

Terry ran forward, grabbed the black key on a diving roll and launched himself into the air as the sword reformed. He smashed it against the back of the construct's head with all of his weight behind it. He bounced against the golem's back and threw himself away as another explosion slammed into its chest.

Landing a few feet away, Terry bared his teeth at the construct and raised the black sword in his right hand and the white key in his left. "Come on, Tiny. You've only got a couple of shots left. Why don't you take 'em?"

The construct swung at him with its remaining fist and Terry struck at the spiderweb of cracks spreading across its elbow. The massive hand crashed into Terry's chest as his blade sent a shower of splintered shards of the construct's armor out into the parking lot. Terry grunted and rolled with the blow. He could barely feel the impact as his body slid across the charred pavement. He smiled as he raised the black blade again and brought it down across the construct's elbow a second time.

The fist dropped to the ground as the entire arm shattered under the impact. Terry took a deep breath, drawing in the leaking power from the smoking ruins of the construct's stump of an arm. As the power slid through him, his body began to feel both lighter and sturdier. His skin felt like it was pulsing with warmth, and he let himself take a step back and marvel at it.

The construct twisted at the hips and swung its left arm with what was left of its strength. Terry found himself soaring upward over the parking lot. He looked down at the construct's raised cannon, energy pooling at its end. There wasn't anywhere for him to go, nothing for him to do. The blast of pure, blinding energy tore through the air and all Terry could do was let it come.

Instincts and training took control of his mind. He stabbed forward with the black blade, drawing the power of the blast in as he fell. Pain traced its way like a ball up his right arm. The muscles and bones tore themselves apart as the massive influx of energy shredded its way through his nerves then reknit themselves back together with power drained from the blast.

The ball of tearing pain screamed slowly up his arm, into his shoulders and across his chest. He pushed it back down his left arm, forcing the energy down into his hand. The white key dangled from his wrist when he let it go to form his hand into the rough resemblance of a gun.

He compressed all of the power from the two inch beam down into a single marble, took aim, and clicked his thumb like a hammer. Raw force exploded out of his fingertips, crashed against the construct's weakened chest, and kept on going. A ten foot hole erupted in the parking lot and the construct fell back into it as the light faded from its eyes.

Terry hit the ground and dropped to one knee. He couldn't feel his left hand, but he could see the flesh already regenerating over the exposed bones at the tips of his fingers. The white key dangled below his hand, glowing softly. He watched as the skin finally formed back over the muscle. Blood rushed back into his hand and he shook away the tingling, sleepy sensation.

Sirens echoed in the near distance and flashing red lights appeared at the end of the street. Terry looked over at the colonel standing quietly to the side of the parking lot, mouth open and eyes wide. He slipped the two keys back around his neck as he approached the older man. He set his jaw and starred with hard eyes.

Slate stepped in between them. "Colonel, you'd better call some PR guy before the news's crews show up, right? You don't want to have to explain any of this yourself."

The colonel nodded and climbed up into the truck. He pulled a cell phone from his pocket and began barking orders to someone on the other end. Terry nodded to Slate, content to let him handle the politics. He turned his attention to Leigh who was digging in the ruins of the construct.

She climbed up from the hole holding the last two stones. "We do not want to leave these here," she said. "Make nuclear bombs look like firecrackers, remember?"

"You gonna lock them in storage again?" Terry asked. He pulled a cigarette from his pocket and lit it. "Do this all over again in a few years?"

Leigh shook her head then nodded toward the slick black armor standing at the edge of the lot. "Nope, I'm going to give my girl some upgrades. I think she could run for months on one of these."

They stood there for a few moments, Terry quietly smoking, Leigh pulling other pieces from Tiny's ruins. When the ambulance pulled into the driveway, Slate directed them to where David had managed to stabilize Roderick. They both got loaded into the back by the EMTs and sped away.

Terry finished his cigarette and climbed into the driver's seat of his car, suddenly exhausted. He turned over the engine and leaned back in the seat with a yawn.

"I told you! You did need the big one," Munindwade said as they pulled out of the parking lot and left the mayhem behind them.

CHAPTER 28

Terry sat in the waiting room at Cox South making notes in his journal. He sighed and sat the book down in the empty chair beside him and turned his attention to the television on the wall. A news report was covering the most recent press conference from one Senator or another. The new registration laws were controversial. Magi-tech was out there, now, and it would take a lot more than a handful of regulations to change that.

"What do you think," he asked Leigh sitting a few seats down. "Should the government be more involved in regulating the magic industry or is that just one more grab for power by a bloated federal system?"

"I think regulation would cut into profits and that would be bad for private industry," she said. She pushed a button on the edge of the tablet, closed the case, and slid it down into her bag. "And there's another mouth to feed now. We'll need all the profits we can handle."

"Oh, good. Because I thought you'd fall on the side of "no death robots" but clearly, I'm mistaken."

"There isn't another mouth to feed yet," Suez complained from his seat across the waiting room. "How long do babies take, anyway? We've been here for nine hours already."

Gabriel gave him a squeeze. "I imagine it's a lot harder on Trish than it is on us."

Terry hopped to his feet and pulled a pack of cigarettes from his pocket. "I'm going outside for a nice healthy treat. Anyone want to come?" He waited for a couple of seconds as everyone shook their heads. "Suit yourselves."

He walked out of the waiting area and headed down the hall of the maternity wing to the stairs. He stopped next to the sign showing the burn ward one floor up. Roderick was right above them, slowly recovering. David had worked miracles on him, but there was only so much the human body could recover from completely. He'd have scars, but he'd live. In a few months, he'd probably even be back at work.

Terry took a deep breath and pushed open the door to the stairs and headed up. The ward was off limits to the general public and he had to wait for someone to come through the door before he could dart inside. It didn't take him long to find the room he was looking for. The black-suited guard standing outside made it easy.

Terry flashed his badge to the guy, and was surprised when he was allowed in. He hadn't expected it to work and had only the vaguest idea of what to do now that it did. He stood inside the door, just watching Roderick breathe. His friend, at least the man who he thought was his friend, was covered almost entirely from head-to-toe with clean bandages. His eyes watched Terry, alert and full of fear.

"I'm not going to kill you, Roddy." Terry pulled a chair from the corner of the room over to sit next to the bed. "I know you think I'm a monster. That's harsh, but I understand."

He leaned back and watched Roderick's eyes. When the engineer finally began to relax, he pulled a sharpie from his pocket. "Want me to sign your cast? Blink twice for yes."

Roderick rolled his eyes, but blinked twice. Terry stood up, and leaned forward. He scribbled several symbols onto the bandages at roughly the center of Roderick's forehead. "You see, Max. I thought we were friends. I genuinely liked you. I think I could still like you. But, you know something very, very dangerous. The easiest solution would be for me to kill you."

He stood back up and touched the fingers of his right hand to the symbols. "I mean, it would be really easy for me to kill you. But, I'm not a murderer. I'm not like you." He took a deep breath and focused a bit of power into the symbols. They blazed to life in a soft glow and slowly sunk down through the bandages. Roderick's eyes widened and he moaned as the spell sank down into his brain, but his heart never spiked. He never felt any actual pain.

"Now, you won't have to worry about that. Just forget, Roddy. Forget everything about the stones and the construct. Forget and never remember."

Terry clicked the lid back on the sharpie and stuck it back in his pocket. He could feel the magic still working inside Roderick's mind, cutting away parts of his memory, burning away others. He knew that when

157

it was done, Max would just wake up, himself. No memories of what the stones were or how they worked. Leigh had proven it worked, even if she'd put too much behind the wall.

He left the room without saying anything to the guard outside and slipped back out into the stairwell.

"There you are!" Gabriel said from below him. "Come on, David wants you to meet his son."

Thank You for Reading

Did you enjoy reading Fallout? Indie authors survive by the strength of their reviews. If you enjoyed Choices, please leave a review and let me and other readers know!

GET FREE SHORT STORIES

Would you like access to **FREE** Short Stories by M.A. Brotherton?

OF COURSE YOU WOULD!

Click or visit the link below for exclusive stories, bonuses, sales, and FREE SHORT STORIES just for signing up!

SIGN UP HERE:
http://mabrotherton.com/newsletter/

OTHER BOOKS BY
M.A. BROTHERTON

SEVEN KEYS SAGA
Book One: Choices
Book Two: Fallout
Book Three: Summons
Book Four: Tragedy

ABSURD SCIENCE FICTION
Dinosaur Alien Invasion
Alcohologist Chronicles

Click or Visit the Link Below for Even More:
Http://mabrotherton.com/books

About the Author

M.A. Brotherton is a writer, blogger, artist, and fat-kid from the suburbs of Kansas City, Missouri. He's tasted a little bit of everything the Midwest has to offer, ranging from meth-tweaking rednecks in massive underground cave complexes to those legendary amber waves of grain. When he's not writing, he spends most of his time on twitter (@MABrotherton) and Facebook, blogging on his website (http://www.mabrotherton.com), or participating in his favorite LARP.

Drop him an email. He looks forward to hearing from you!

www.ingramcontent.com/pod-product-compliance
Lightning Source LLC
Chambersburg PA
CBHW021157130626
46554CB00005B/1867